To Lead Us Home

Ben's Tale

I0633784

Dorothy M Mitchell

chipmunkapublishing
the mental health publisher

Published by
Chipmunkapublishing
PO Box 6872
Brentwood
Essex CM13 1ZT
United Kingdom

http://www.chipmunkapublishing.com

Edited by Lucy Lythgoe

ISBN 978-1-84991-766-7

Chipmunkapublishing gratefully acknowledge the support of Arts Council England.

AUTHOR BIOGRAPHY

Dorothy was born in a small village in Yorkshire just before the Second World War. She remembers they were hard times. She remembers being in the air-raid shelter in the garden. Being in there at night as enemy bombs rained down wasn't very pleasant. At the age of six she didn't really understand what it was all about, but she did understand the sweet shop having lots of empty sweet jars.

She remembers her mum swapping coupons with other mothers. Sugar coupons for clothing coupons, was a regular occurrence.

Dorothy left Yorkshire when she was sixteen, and moved with her family to Evesham in 1954. Her dad had got employment as steward of a social club. Dorothy sometimes helped her dad, in the club. This was where she met the man who was to become her husband. She married at the age of eighteen, much too young as far as her mother was concerned, but Dorothy was married to Joe for thirty-six years. She had her first son Andrew at the age of twenty-one, and her second son David when she was twenty -seven.

Joe died at the age of fifty-eight after a long illness, and Dorothy was devastated. Her boys were very good but they both had their own lives to lead.

Dorothy was asked by a friend about eighteen months after the death to accompany her to her church. Her feelings at that sad time were 'Well I can't feel any worse than I do right now' so she went the following Sunday evening. To her surprise Dorothy found comfort from the service and to cut a long story short, Dorothy met, and fell in love with Ken, who attended the church. Everyone there was concerned for him. He had lost his wife to illness about a year before she was widowed. Ken was going down in his health and the church people where concerned about him. Well that was a long time ago. Dorothy and Ken have been married for almost eighteen happy years.

Dorothy was diagnosed with Multiple Sclerosis when she was thirty-seven. She has suffered many relapses and has seen the inside of a few hospitals.

About fifteen years ago Dorothy realised she had a flare for writing, and to date she has had many poems published but the most exciting thing to happen was when CHIPMUNKA PUBLISHING picked her up. Dorothy now has three novels under her belt with more on the way. "To see my work being sold by CHIPMUNKA PUBLISHING, WATERSTONES and AMAZON is almost unbelievable. My thanks go to my sons Andrew and David, my husband Ken, my Grandson Ben and my good friend Martin P Buckley for their help and patience".

PREFACE

This is the story of Ben the useless Border Collie! Well that's what his first owner Gwyn Thomas thought. The sheep farmer had suffered a mental breakdown at the time. He had lost his wife in a terrible accident, causing him to almost lose his mind! This had culminated in him almost giving up the struggle. His daughter Belle had also been involved in the tragedy, having her arm so badly injured it had had to be removed. Ben had been her pet, but he was also supposed to be a sheep dog, helping his mum Floss to take care of the large flock. Unfortunately, Ben had been born with a weak back leg, making it almost impossible for him to control the sheep. He was ok on a straight run, but when it came to turning round his leg let him down, causing the poor dog to fall over. It always upset him, but there was nothing he could do to alter the situation try as he might.

Now ordinarily. Gwyn Thomas would have overlooked this fact, and allowed his daughter to keep the young dog, however, because of his then embittered, twisted state of mind Ben had been sent away to kennels, and an uncertain future, leaving Belle and his mother Floss almost heartbroken at his going.

This heartwarming tale is full of danger and love, it tells of many hair-raising happenings. It is told by Ben; most of the time, from his perspective. Some people don't believe dogs can understand much about human beings or that dogs can have feelings, but let me assure you that this simply isn't true. This story will tell you dogs know much more than some people realize. The story speaks of the many harrowing trials Ben encounters during his long journey before he reaches what to him is home. He endures beatings from the deranged kennel owner, who takes out his frustrations on dogs that are supposed to be in his care. Ben also experiences real love from people like Belle Thomas. She was the daughter of the farmer Gwyn Thomas. Also to be given a mention, is warm-hearted but over stretched kennel maid, Peggy Owen, who worked at Glynloyd Kennel. She suffered much at the hands of the kennel owner, Jake Binley.

Read about Ben's mum Floss, and Nellie the Golden Labrador, and Peggy Owen who are all so important in the telling of this lovely tale. They are definitely the loves of this Collie's life!

Please read and enjoy the riveting, sometimes funny, sometimes sad, heart warming adventure.

CHAPTER ONE

LEAVING HOME

Belle held her breath, she was just finishing her breakfast, she couldn't believe what she was hearing. Her dad was in the yard talking to Mr. Walker from the next-door farm.

"The dog's useless Burt, absolutely useless. He'll never make a good sheepdog, more's the pity! I had hoped that a pup of Floss's would follow in her footsteps, the best Sheep Dog I have ever known! But no! It wasn't to be, the weak back leg means Ben's fine on a straight run but no good on the turn and I can't afford to carry any more dead weight. He's a nice enough dog Burt, I'll give you that but nice doesn't pay the bills. Besides, with all the sheep trials, taking Floss here there and everywhere, I just haven't got the time. The farm doesn't run itself you know Burt."

Belle heard Mr. Walker say something about keeping Ben for breeding but her dad had said no.
"I haven't got the time or inclination for all that besides, how do I know that the dog won't pass on the weakness? No the dog has got to go, and that's all there is to say on the matter."
Belle heard Mr. Walker's gruff voice, pleading with her dad. She liked Mr. Walker. He always called her Tinkerbell".

"The lass will take it hard Gwyn: you know how she dotes on the Collie.
You will break her heart if the dog is sent away, and you know how she is since the accident; losing her mother and her arm can't be easy for the girl, she loves Ben. He was her comfort at that terrible time. Don't do this to her Gwyn there must be another way round this man"?

Belle heard her dad groan but Mr. Walker carried on pursuing his argument.

"Don't take out your own heartbreak on the young girl for pity's sake Gwyn."

Belle heard her dad's voice change.

"It's no good you trying to change things Burt, I've made my mind up. He's going tomorrow evening, Glynloyd Kennels are taking him."

Burt Walker trying in vain to make Gwyn change his mind said:

"I know things have been hard for you since Miriam died in the car smash; it was one hell of a shock, but think of your daughter for pity's sake man. She is ten years old, and to lose her mum and most of her left arm can't be easy for her; and now you want to take her pet, you are asking too much of the lass."

Belle heard a loud noise. It was Gwyn smashing the kitchen door with his fist,

and in an equally angry sounding voice he shouted:

"She can have a hamster or tortoise if she likes but the dog isn't her pet; he's going, and that is all I am saying on the subject Burt, now if you'll excuse me." With that Gwyn Thomas left the yard, and walked into the farm kitchen.

Belle looked at her dad, he had changed so much since the car accident. He used to be lovely, but not any more. Oh he looked after her, held her when the pain of the loss was unbearable, the memories of the crash came to torment her at night. He tended to her when her stump had given her real pain. But the nice dad had gone to be replaced by an almost stranger. She missed her mum too. Life just wasn't the same without her.

There seemed to be an emptyness inside, a frightening hole that nothing could fill.

Belle had asked herself many times a question that was impossible to answer.
Did her dad blame her for pestering to go to the last Sheep Dog Trials? It had only been over the hill at Long Acres Farm, not miles away like some of the trials. Besides, her Mum had wanted to make a day of it. The weather had been nice on that particular day so it was decided that Miriam and Belle would travel in her dad's little run around. They would follow behind Gwyn in the trailer that was carrying Floss. They had arrived all right and were able to witness Floss winning yet another rosette for best in her class.

It was on the way home that the accident that was to change life forever happened. Somehow Miriam got caught up on a patch of oil. She lost control of the car, and skidded down an embankment. She was killed instantly, Belle sustaining a terrible injury to her arm, meaning lots of hospital visits. She had been lucky, well, that's what people said, but had she? Her dad was a changed man, Miriam was dead, and she had lost almost half her left arm.

Ben had helped when she came out of hospital after being in for an operation to tidy up the stump after the horrible car crash that had left her crippled and without her mum. She would find comfort cuddling the young Collie when things had been bad, his soft fur and warm body giving comfort where there was none. It was as if some instinct told the dog that something really bad had happened. Belle had talked to Ben and cried to him so of course the young dog had picked up on the sadness.

Well it was more than instinct! Ben had known something awful had happened when there was talk of an accident involving Belle and her mum. He knew Mrs Thomas had been killed and Belle had lost some of her arm. He loved Belle, she had treated him like her pet ever since it was realized that he would never make a good sheep dog. True he wasn't able to speak to her but he knew a lot more about what went on around Hilltop's Farm than most people gave him credit for. He knew Belle had loved him since he had been a tiny pup. He was also aware, that his time on Hilltop's was hanging in the balance. Perhaps if Miriam Thomas hadn't been killed and Belle crippled in that terrible accident a couple of months ago, things may have been different.

Ben remembered his master had been happy back then. Always whistling and singing, Ben reckoned the singing wasn't up to much, but it was a joyful sound so it hadn't mattered that a few notes were as flat as a pancake. Well that was what he remembered Miriam saying.

However since the terrible day of the car smash, Miriam being killed outright, and Belle losing her arm, the life that used to be, had gone out of his master. Things hadn't been the same and as far as Ben could make out, they never would be again.

Ben was upset that he couldn't do a better job with the sheep and he had really tried to control those stupid beasts, but try as he might, he just couldn't get the hang of it.
His back leg let him down every time. He was ok on a straight run, but when it came to turning, he fell over. Ben knew he was letting his boss down, but he couldn't help it.

He had watched his mum Floss. She was brilliant, always managing to get the sheep to do just as Gwyn wanted them to do. He was so proud of her, she was brilliant, winning at sheep dog trials all over the place but sadly, he knew with a certainty, that he would never be good with the sheep.

Gwyn carried on pressing his point. "He's got to go Belle, and that's all there is to it, no good you sitting there moaning about the fact. We just can't afford to keep him any longer and let that be the end of the matter."

Belle, not wanting to give in responded: "but Dad! It's so cruel, Ben is only a puppy, he will miss us and be upset, please Dad let him stay here with us on the farm where he belongs, please."

Gwyn, in a raised voice, sounding very angry now, replied:
"I know girl; and it's very sad; but I run a business here, not a dogs' home. Ben will never be any good with the sheep. A weak back leg lets him down on the turn every time. I've watched him so I know. True it's not his fault Belle No-no, but I have to be sensible lass, he is costing me money and as far as I can see it is wasted cash that I could put to better use."

Then the farmer seeing the upset in his girl's eyes, tried to placate her but it was a poor effort on his part. He seemed to have lost all the softness he once possessed. Gwyn Thomas was a broken man.

"He is no good to me as a working dog. The sheep run rings round him, and I can't afford to keep him on as a pet for you my girl so just put that idea out of your head once and for all, besides: I have enough on my plate now what with your mum gone and you with only one good arm. It's not your fault I know but the farm won't run itself, life is hard girl very hard, so you had better get used to it."

Tears of anguish began to run down the girl's face, and not ready to give up she continued to plead with Gwyn:

"but Dad, Ben isn't a year old yet and he loves us. You can't do this Dad; you just can't, Ben loves me and I love Ben."

The farmer, fed up with the argument finally lost his temper.

He turned to his daughter:

"Now that's enough about the damn dog; he's not your pet, despite what you and Burt Walters might think; he's going and that's all I'm going to say on the subject; he's going today, and that's the end of it. The Glynloyd kennels are taking him; I'm driving him over this evening, so you had better get used to the idea and say your goodbye now".   With that, the angry farmer stormed out of the house, muttering to himself as he went.

Belle was sobbing now, her good arm tight around my neck. To tell the truth I wasn't feeling all that good, so it was true then, all I had known was about to change. I was going to be taken away from my lovely home on Hilltop's Farm, away from my mum Floss, and Belle who both love me. Belle needed me now, since the terrible car accident. Why was this happening? I was about to be taken to a strange new place and there wasn't a thing I could do to stop it.

I'm Ben by the way. The useless Border Collie Dog. Well, that's according to my master Gwyn Thomas. I thought he cared for me a bit. I do my best to please him. It isn't my fault that one of my back legs is weak. After all I was born with it. I didn't choose to be like this.

I was feeling very scared now and I don't mind admitting it; whatever was to become of me? I could feel my legs starting to shake. I was more frightened than I had ever been in my life. Belle, who was sobbing quietly now, was holding me so tight I could hardly breathe. Her tears were making my coat wet. Suddenly I wanted my mum: yes; I must go and find my mum: she would know what to do. These were my anxious thoughts as I pulled away from Belle.

No more cuddling on the sweet hay with Floss my lovely mum and no more playing with Belle who had claimed me as her own pet when Mum was working with the sheep? I felt a shiver run through my body. "Oh Mum, what is going to happen to me now"?

I had struggled free from the weeping girl. This was a nightmare. I ran as fast as my legs would carry me to the barn where I knew I would find comfort with my lovely mother.

Floss had been expecting her boy. She had heard talk between Gwyn and Walter Standish who worked on one of the farms in the area near to Hilltop's. She had waited for this sad day to arrive and now it was here. She recognized Ben's footfall and his gasping breath as the pup ran alongside the barn.

I was almost spent with exhaustion but I would soon be with Mum. I rushed towards the door. I ran inside and stopped for a split second. After my eyes became accustomed to the dark I heaved a sigh of relief. Floss my mum would make everything right now!
There she was, my lovely mother. I rushed towards her.

"Mum have you heard the news?" Gwyn is sending me away; please Mum; don't let him do it. I live here with you and Belle, I will try harder to make my back leg stronger so I can come chasing those daft sheep with you. Mum please help me, I don't want to leave you and

Belle, please Mum, I am frightened and my tummy feels upset; Belle needs me, don't let them take me."

I waited for Mum to give me some comfort. She always had in the past but with heart pounding, I knew Mum couldn't help me; not this time. She had covered for me when I had fallen over at times whilst turning round chasing the stupid sheep. My leg was weak and there was no getting away from that fact. I would never make a good sheep dog and Gwyn Thomas knew it.

It was the way of things on a sheep farm. Nellie my girl friend had been sent away a few weeks earlier. She was a lovely Golden Labrador; about the same age as me. Gwyn said she was too timid to be a farm dog but she was lovely. I miss her a lot, and I don't think I will ever see her again. We used to have fun, chasing round the haystacks, and barking at the hens and geese and getting up to mischief. I don't understand any of this. Everything is just horrible.

Belle is lovely, but she isn't a dog. Even she doesn't understand the importance of rolling in cow muck. Nellie and I used to love that. Nellie was great; she understood everything. She knew the need to get stuck into a pile of fresh smelly cow dung and what about fox muck! My Oh my! Now that was something else. A real treat you may say. I think Nellie enjoyed the aroma of fox poo better than I did. Nellie was great. I heaved a sigh of sadness. Life as I had known it was finished. I felt another tear run down my face and drip from the end of my nose.

Floss looked at her boy, and felt helpless. But she knew in order to help Ben she must try to make him understand. It was going to be the hardest thing she had ever done in her life, but she must do her best in order to help her pup.

Floss responded in the gentlest voice she could muster:
"now Ben; you know the way of it, every dog has to leave his mother one day. I realize it is going to be very hard, for both of us; but we must be strong. Mum nuzzled me once more.

I listened to what my mum was saying, but I didn't like the sound of it one bit.
I answered her with a tremble in my voice.

"But why do I have to leave you, I don't want to go. I want to stay on the farm with you and Belle, couldn't I be a guard dog?" I knew I was clutching at straws, but I so wanted to stay on Hilltop's Farm.

Floss, in a quiet voice said, "now listen to me my son. You are almost a full-grown Collie now, and it's your time to leave; no use you trying to avoid it. You must be a very brave dog." Try to keep in your heart everything I have taught you. Don't let me down, but most important, don't let yourself down, always be a good dog.

By this time I was crying uncontrollably. I could hear mum talking but I didn't want to listen to these sad words.

Floss noting the pain her pup was suffering, nuzzled his neck once more,
"now come on my son, be brave and try to look on this as an adventure."

I was listening to the words my mum was speaking; I tried to snuggle as close as I could into her soft coat. This was awful. I just wanted to stay safe here with my lovely mum forever but with a cold grip of fear that had enveloped me I realized this was not going to be.

I felt mum pull away and in a soft voice, she said. "remember I will always love you, be a good dog; you are about to start a new chapter in your life. Be brave my son and try to look on this as an adventure."

Just then I heard quick footsteps coming towards me, also an urgent, whispered voice.
"Ben, Ben." It was Belle. "Come on boy". A weeping Belle tugged at my collar. "Come with me, I won't let anybody take you away from Hilltop's."
With difficulty she secured a piece of string around my collar then by holding one end in her mouth she managed to tie a knot. It was rather uncomfortable. Before I knew it I was being whisked away. I was being half dragged and half pulled by Belle.
"Come on boy before anyone sees us. I know a place we can hide where nobody will ever find us." Belle spoke to my mum. "Try not to worry Floss, Ben and I will be alright, I can't let him be taken away."

I was running with Belle, She was carrying a heavy bag. My spirits lifted a little. Perhaps things were looking up. I didn't like the idea of leaving my mum again, but if Belle could help, then I was all for it so with renewed vigour I tried to run my hardest.

We left the bottom yard, there was nobody about except for a few hens, the goose, and Dripping the pig. I liked the pig. He was funny. He used to have a mate called Lard, but she had been gone for quite a while. She was ok, a bit snooty though. I preferred Dripping. He could be very droll, but witty. I had never known a pig that could escape from his sty quite as often as Dripping had done just lately. He was one clever pig. Nellie reckoned he was looking for Lard but all the time I was at Hilltop's Farm, he never did find his mate.

I remember Gwyn saying she was a lovely pig, and he was looking forward to a bacon sandwich when she had been seen to.   Whatever that meant!

We kept running, we were now just past the top cornfield.
"Come on Ben, we must get away before Dad gets home." Eventually we left Hilltop's Farm, and Belle, still pulling me, headed for the brook.   By now the warm sun that had been shining for most of the day was being replaced by a shower of rain, a shower that soon turned into a deluge.   As we ran I could feel my bad leg beginning to ache. Belle was puffing and panting. I knew we must stop for a rest very soon. We were approaching Bluebell Woods and the brook. I loved this place, Belle used to take Nellie and me for our walks in this wood when we were still together. We still came for walks here, Belle and I, but it had never been quite the same since Gwyn sent my Nellie away.

We must have run about a mile by now. I knew this because Gwyn had told Belle off for going too far when she had taken us for a long walk once. By now I was feeling tired and very thirsty. Belle was slowing down also, she must have been feeling tired as well.

In a panting voice Belle who had just loosened the uncomfortable string, said to me, "go and find the stream Ben it can't be far away, we are getting near to Badgers' Brook."

I did as Belle told me, by now we were both very wet, I didn't like the rain much. It made my thick coat feel heavy but I needed a drink. Just then a clap of thunder ripped the air. I didn't like thunder; Mum used to hide me under her coat until a storm had passed. I breathed a deep tremulous sigh. I didn't think at this point in time, that I would ever feel real comfort again.

I found the stream, swollen now since the heavy rainstorm. I took a welcome drink. Heavy rain had swelled the brook already. Belle kneeled down on the wet ground and cupping her hands she filled the make shift vessel with water from the brook. She took a drink. Belle looked as wet as I felt. After a few moments we set off once more. We had reached the edge of Bluebell Wood. By now it was getting dark. After what seemed a long time, Belle stopped and in a tired voice said "come on Ben we are here, nobody will find us now."

I looked around me and all I could see were trees and more trees.
"This way Ben, follow me." I kept as close as I could to Belle. After what seemed an age, we arrived at a very large tree.
"Come on Ben round the back." I followed Belle as closely as I could. I was soaking wet and very cold. My thick coat felt heavy, Belle was as wet as I was.

The tree was one of the biggest I had ever seen. When we got to the back I was intrigued to see a large hole just above ground level.

Belle pushed me inside, and followed behind. By the smell coming from inside it was evident that the large tree hole had been home to a fox at some time. When my eyes grew accustomed to the dark, I realized that this space was quite big enough to hide us both.

Belle sat down beside me and after getting her breath she removed her dress wrung out as much rain water as she could considering she only had one good arm, and hung it on a knobbled lump of wood sticking out just to the side of us. After trying to dry me with the bits of twig and debris from the floor inside the tree, which didn't really work, she opened the heavy bag she had been carrying.

From inside Belle brought out a newspaper parcel. As she opened it the aroma of strong cheese teased my nostrils. Belle pulled out a chunk of bread, a wedge of the delicious smelly cheese, and a tin of my favourite dog food.
My mouth began to salivate. I felt really hungry. I was given a piece of cheese. As I wolfed it down, dogs do that, I wondered why Belle seemed to be upset. She was searching the bag franticly.
"Oh Ben would you believe it, in my hurry to get away from Hilltop's I forgot to bring a tin- opener."

I was still savouring the taste of that lovely cheese. Belle seemed to slump. "What am I going to give you now?" How could I tell Belle dogs can look after their tummies if need be. I knew how to catch a rabbit, that was one thing Mum had taught me. If you were very careful it wasn't that difficult to catch a bunny that was busily eating a juicy carrot.

I remembered the rabbit that Nellie and I shared once. Mind you, it was my girlfriend's catch, she was much quicker than me. I never cared for the taste of raw rabbit, but I wouldn't say no to a meal of bunny at the moment, although I am more used to biscuits and cooked food.

Belle picked up a handful of dry scrub from inside the trunk. She began to rub my wet coat once more but it was no good. The twigs and debris got stuck in my still sodden fur. Eventually she gave up. "Come on Ben why don't we cuddle up, we will soon get dry. I was more than willing to snuggle up with Belle, I settled down exhausted in her arms.

Soon the girl and dog fell fast asleep. Meanwhile back at Hilltop's Farm. Gwyn Thomas was becoming increasingly worried. He couldn't find Belle or the damn dog. It was evening and by now he should be halfway to Glynloyd Kennels. Gwyn cursed under his breath. The blasted Collie is more trouble than he's worth." When it eventually became obvious that neither Belle nor the dog where anywhere to be found, the farmer became really worried.

Gwyn rang Burt Walters. "Can you give me a hand Burt! The girl and the dog have done a runner." Burt not surprised by the news, assured the farmer that the pair wouldn't have gone very far. "I'll be with you in about half an hour."

By now it was pitch black. The rain was still pouring in torrents. Burt arrived in his land rover.

He stepped out into the yard, and ran to the farmhouse, to discover a very agitated farmer, waiting for him.
"Can't see hide nor hair of them Burt. Where the hell can they be?"
Burt, shaking the rain from his cap replied "have you looked in the barns, and milking sheds"? Gwyn nodded, "Aye and the pigsty and cold cellar?"
Burt shook his head.
"Well it's safe to say that the lass has taken the dog! She didn't want to lose him Gwyn, that's about it. I think you had better ring the police, don't you?"

Gwyn Thomas, angry but by now very worried decided that getting in touch with the police was the only option left to him.

After phoning the police station, the men waited. Eventually a car squelched into the wet farmyard and came to a halt. Two officers got out, and hurried to the farmhouse. On gaining entrance they removed their helmets and wiped rain from their faces.

Gwyn showed them to a couple of chairs. Both men sat down. One of the officers took a notepad from his pocket. After blowing his nose loudly on a not too clean handkerchief, he addressed Gwyn:
"now sir can you tell me the approximate time the girl and dog went missing?"
Gwyn after thinking for a moment responded, "not sure officer, could be an hour could be longer". He continued, "I was in the top field for quite a long time; one of the sheep had slipped into the ditch; I had a hell of a job with her, so it was probably longer than I first thought."

The police officer took a few more notes. "You say you checked the barns and out-buildings?" Gwyn Nodded. After a few more minutes, both men stood up. The other policeman who hadn't spoken yet just kept his eyes on Gwyn.

"If you don't mind Sir, we will take another look"
Gwyn , feeling rather anxious said. "I have already told you officer; they are not on the farm, if they had been I would have found them."

Well the thing is, policemen are naturally suspicious, and not happy with the answers given. They decided to conduct their own search.
Gwyn by now was almost tearing his hair out by the roots and said angrily:
"for pity's sake man; my daughter is not on the farm, how many more times, this is all because she wanted to keep that good-for-nothing dog."

The policemen looked at one another. They were aware of the trauma this particular farmer had endured. In fact the officer who took the notes had been present when the wife had been killed in the car accident. He remembered well the terrible arm injury sustained by the girl. If the farmer was unhitched in his mind owing to the accident, then who knows what had happened to the girl and dog? Strange minds can do strange things.

One of the officers glanced at his watch. "10.35 p.m. We can't conduct a search tonight. For one thing it's too dark to see anything, and another, in this thunderstorm we won't be able to make any headway. The police officers stood up, replaced their helmets, and with a promise to begin the search at first light, they left Hilltop's farm.

By now most of the surrounding farms and hamlets had heard about Belle Thomas and the dog going missing. Burt Walters had a lovely caring wife, but unfortunately Mabel Walters had been born with the gift of the gab so it wasn't long before the news of the disappearance had spread.

At first light the following morning, as promised the two policemen who had attended the previous evening arrived at the farm in their police car. They were followed closely by a number of people from neighboring farms who, had heard about the missing girl and dog from Mabel Walter's urgent phone calls; Mabel was nosy, but caring.

After a few words as to where to begin the search, it was decided that owing to the fact that there were about a dozen people eager to find the missing pair, the police decided to split them into groups of four. Making sure that there was a gun to each group, the police officer gave instructions to the searchers:

"If you find them; give one blast of your gun into the air, and stay there until the rest of the party arrive on the scene."

So with clear instructions from the police officer, the search parties set off. Gwyn Thomas, after a sleepless night was relieved that at last help was at hand. The farmer followed closely behind the police. He had collected Floss from the barn. If anybody could find the missing pair it was the dog's mother. Gwyn had so wanted to begin the search last night but he had to admit that it wouldn't have been a good idea.

The thunderstorm had been ferocious, not fit for man nor beast but Gwyn had suffered much heartache and torment. He should have been looking for his girl. She was out in the storm somewhere, all because of that darn dog! By now the storm that had raged most of the previous night had blown itself out. The ground was still sopping wet. There were deep tyre-tracks where vehicles had come in and out of the farmyard.

Floss pulled hard on the lead. She had picked up that something bad had happened. Ever since the distraught Belle had come into the barn and pulled Ben away from her side she knew something awful would come of it, so with urgency she pulled hard on the lead holding her. The three search parties had gone in different directions. One search party, had gone to the sight of the Old Water Mill down by Badgers' Brook, swollen now since last night's storm. Another group concentrated their search along the sight of the Black Bridge, a very dangerous place. Gwyn had warned Belle long ago to never go anywhere near the bridge. The farmer remembered an accident there. He recalled the train, and the lad who lost his life. No. Belle wouldn't be anywhere near the bridge.

Gwyn and Floss were with the first group. Floss, who had been keeping her nose close to the wet ground, suddenly stopped. Gwyn anxious asked, "What is it girl, can you smell something?"

The Collie, picked up her right front paw, stood motionless, stuck her nose in the air, gave a whine and pulled strongly on the lead.

Gwyn quick as a flash released Floss. She was a good dog, and if anyone could find the missing girl and Ben it would be Floss. This was true. Floss had worried ever since Belle had whisked her pup away yesterday. She was well aware just how much the girl loved her boy but this had been a foolish thing to do.

Floss ran towards Bluebell Wood, picking up speed as she went. Gwyn called out. "Wait for me girl" but the dog pressed on oblivious to her master's call.

Gwyn eventually caught up with the Collie. Floss was sniffing close to the ground near to a large oak tree. She had found the missing pair. Belle was curled up seemingly asleep in a large hole in the trunk of the big oak tree and Ben was sitting near-by tucking into a rabbit that he had caught.

The police officer who was in charge of the group, fired his shot gun into the air. He and Gwyn, after finding Belle, realized that the girl had a chill, due no doubt to being out all night in the thunderstorm. They lifted her out from inside the mighty oak tree and very quickly carried her home.

When Belle was tucked up in her warm bed and Dr Harding had given her medication Gwyn allowed himself to breathe a sigh of relief. Meanwhile Ben had been allowed to stay in the barn with his mother for one more night.   Not a reprieve, oh no! This episode had determined Gwyn that his decision to get rid of the Collie had been correct.

Ben had cuddled up to his mum, He was feeling more upset than he thought. He had spent another night with Floss but he knew she was sad about Belle's decision to run away. She spoke sadly to her pup.
"You could have been killed the pair of you, trees came down last night in the storm and now Belle has a touch of something called bronchitis. I heard Gwyn telling Burt. He said he was taking you to Glynloyd this evening."
Floss snuggled her nose into Ben's neck. It had been wonderful to spend another night with her boy. However, this time there was no going back. She had probably spent the last night ever with her Ben but this was the end of the line.

Ben could feel himself begin to tremble. This was it. The sheep were all in the bottom field; it was evening, and I knew what that meant. I didn't want to go. I cried out; "Mum Oh Mum please don't let them take me" and I nuzzled into her warm neck for comfort once more.   I heard footsteps coming towards the barn. The doors opened.
Gwyn Thomas came in and walked quickly over to where I was snuggling up to Mum. "Come on now dog; No more of your tricks it's time to go." You've had another night but it will definitely be your last on this farm."

I couldn't move; my world was falling apart.   Mum looked into my eyes.
"Go on son, be a good lad, and remember always how much I love you."

For the rest of my life; I was never going to forget the look of heartbreak my mother couldn't conceal in her gentle eyes.

I knew now with a chilling fear, that I was never going to see my mum again,
and she was aware of that sad fact also. I felt completely and utterly alone.
A strong hand grabbed my collar; "come on you, I am not giving you chance to slip away again."

I screamed "Mum, Mum" but before I knew it, I was outside in the yard. The barn door slammed shut. Gwyn spoke in a gruff angry sounding voice. "Get in the wagon, it's time we were off. It's because of your antics I missed getting rid of you yesterday."

I tried to free myself from his grasp, "Mum, I want my Mum" but despite my wriggling and trying to free myself the farmer was too strong for me. The next moment I was thrown into the back of the wagon. I landed with a bump against what must have been the front of the truck.

This hell on wheels was taking me away to somewhere I didn't want to go, to an uncertain future in a strange place. My heart was beating so fast I could hardly breathe. Mum had told me to be a good lad, but I was scared. This wagon was uncomfortable and noisy. I just sat for a while taking in my surroundings and getting my breath back. The wagon smelled funny, I couldn't see anything. This was horrible. "Mum" I yelled "Mum, please don't let them take me" but it was no use. I was being taken away, by forces stronger than Mum or me. I curled myself into a tight ball of fear and awaited my fate.

As the wagon left the yard, Floss, pent up tears of sorrow flooding her eyes, watched as her pup was being driven away. She whispered sadly. "Goodbye my Son, I will always love you, be brave my little one."

To Lead Us Home

CHAPTER TWO

GLYNLOYD KENNELS

I suppose I must have fallen asleep for the next thing I remember was an unfamiliar voice coming from somewhere close by talking to somebody.

"I thought you were never going to get here" said the voice I didn't like the sound of. It was to turn out later, that I had every right not to like that particular voice, it belonged to a very nasty person by the name of Jake Binley. I was to have many scrapes with that particular gent during my stay at Glynloyd Kennels.

Next I heard Gwyn answer the man with the horrible sounding voice.
"The girl ran off with him yesterday, it took the police and half the folks on the outlying farms searching for 'em. I had a hell of a job to get the blasted mutt off the farm, didn't want to leave his mother, stubborn as they come is this young fella."

The next thing to happen made me jump out of my skin. The back door to the wagon was flung wide open. Gwyn, sounding a bit kinder now, said "come on boy, we're here at long last." I peered out into the darkness. I was in a place completely unknown to me. There was a different smell. I felt cold, and very frightened.

"I've put the kettle on," said the horrible voice. "Thanks mate" said Gwyn. "I could do with a hot drink after the journey I've just had." "Let me see the dog first, have you got his lead?" said Jake Binley.

Gwyn handed over papers that told my new owner all about me: a Welsh-Border Collie, almost one year old with a weak back leg. What it was unable to tell my new owner was just how upset and scared I felt. I wanted my Mum.

"Come here and get this lead on, you're coming with me. You're not playing any of your disappearing tricks on me!" Jake Binley very roughly pulled me along a path, opened a door and shoved me into a dark smelly place. Telling me to be quiet, the door slammed shut and I was alone, very thirsty and very frightened...

When my eyes became accustomed to the dark I could see I was in a small shed. In one corner I could just make out what looked like a bucket. I walked over to it, and saw it was half full of water. I put my head down inside the bucket and sniffed, it didn't smell of anything much, so I put my tongue into the cold liquid. Yes it tasted like water, different from the water I was used to, sort of bitter and stale tasting.

However by this time I was so thirsty, I must have a drink. I began to lap up the funny tasting liquid. I swallowed a soothing mouthful. It seemed ok so I carried on drinking until my thirst was quenched. I must have fallen asleep again. I was awakened in the morning abruptly by barking, howling, yelping and whining. My half-asleep thoughts were that I must be in a mad house. The door of the shed was opened and a bowl of food was placed on the floor in front of me.

"Come on boy; don't be frightened, here is some meat". I looked up to where the voice was coming from. It was a girl. She would be about the same age as my Belle. She had a plump red face, her hair was fair and she wore it in pigtails. I remembered Belle used to have her hair done in the same style sometimes. I sighed at the thought of my Belle back on Hilltop's farm, I suppose she would be missing me by now.

This girl had nice eyes, sort of soft, and kind looking. She pushed the bowl of food a little closer. "Come on lad I won't hurt you, here, have some of this meat." The girl put her hand in the bowl took out a small amount and offered it to me. She was nice; I could sense her gentleness. I stretched forward and took what she was holding. It tasted different from what I was used to but it was meat, and I was starving. I didn't realize just how hungry I was. The meat was surprisingly tasty, not quite what I was used to, but nevertheless I was surprised how much I enjoyed it.

She put her hand out to me again, "come on Boy- I won't hurt you." Some instinct told me that this girl was telling the truth. Very slowly I went towards her. The girl stroked my neck. This bit of comfort gave me confidence. She carried on stroking me, and at the same time made soothing caressing noises with her voice. I felt tears start to well up in my eyes. Probably they were tears of relief. This was after all; the first time I had been shown any kindness since leaving Hilltop's and my lovely mum, and Belle. I felt a pang of anxiety, Oh Mum where are you?

I knew I must be strong and remember what my mum told me. I had to go on without her and Belle now, after all my Nellie had been sent away not long before me. She had to get used to being away from home, just like me. I turned my attention back to the kennel maid.

This girl was a dog person, kind with nice warm eyes. I nuzzled my nose into her other outstretched hand. She smelled of fresh hay and country things and other dogs! The smell reminded me of home, but how could I say home! I knew without a doubt that I would never see Hilltop's ever again or my lovely mum and Belle. They were lost to me forever.

To Lead Us Home

CHAPTER THREE

MAKING FRIENDS

I was soon to learn the extent of Peggy Owen's dislike for Jake Binley, and the reasons why. Binley was the owner of Glynloyd Kennels. Peggy was the kennel maid who I soon found did most of the hard work. Binley however didn't treat the hard working girl any better than he treated us dogs.

I've been living here for about five weeks. I suppose I am getting used to the life at this remote kennels. I still miss my mum, and Belle, but if I have learned anything since being here, it is that my life as I knew it will never come back, and I must do as my mum told me and do my best to be a good dog.

However, I don't think my mum could have known just how hard it was going to be for me. Let me try to explain.

Glynloyd Kennels is situated in a very remote part of North Wales, miles from Hilltop's Farm where I was born. The kennels are situated in a very beautiful but rugged place. The kennels are quite small. There are fourteen pens in all. Most are occupied at the moment by dogs that have been abandoned or lost. Some dogs were only here for a short time whilst their owners were on holiday or ill. I just couldn't imagine any responsible owners leaving their pet in this place by choice! However, I had heard Binley turn on the charm to a gullible pet owner who was looking for somewhere to leave his dog whilst he went on holiday. Little did they know what they were subjecting their pet to! Somewhere down the line however, the truth about Binley and Glynloyd Kennels would one-day surface.

Zebedy lives In the next door pen to me. He is a lovely black Labrador, He comforted me when he could hear my howling the first few nights I arrived at this place. He told me he ended up here when his owner died, and that he understood exactly how I was feeling. He's getting on a bit, but he took me under his wing so to speak, showed me the ropes, and how to keep out of the way of- and also on the right side of horrible Jake Binley.

Zebedy told me this place used to belong to a lady by the name of Pippa Whainright. He doesn't miss anything much, not old Zeb! He keeps his eyes and ears open. He told me the lady had died last year and because she didn't have any surviving relatives, Glynloyd Kennels was put up for auction. Peggy Owen had worked here for years. It was known that Pippa Whainright had been very fond of the girl. Zebedy also told me that people in these parts had been surprised that Glynloyd had not been left to Peggy. Apparently no Will was ever found to support that fact. And this is how Binley got his hands on the Kennels. He kept Peggy on to do the Donkey Work.   There is another young boy by the name of Barry Jones, who helps out at the Kennels, he is a bit simple, and walks with a limp, but is quite kind to us dogs.

Zebedy knows a lot of things, and he's taught me loads of interesting stuff. He is quite old now. Zeb reckons he's about thirteen. I think he is probably right, as I notice his black coat has rather a lot of grey hair.   Zeb is lovely; I am very fond of him.

So I suppose that I am getting used to life in the kennels.   Peggy takes us for long walks every day across the fields. She takes a few of us dogs at a time. Zeb, Charlie, and I, usually go together.   Charlie, well he's what I call a doggy mixture.   He's little with short ginger and white hair and a few black spots dotted here and there. He also has the curliest tail I have ever seen, but oh boy can he run! He is by far the best runner out of the three of us. Apparently according to Charlie, he used to belong to an old lady, she had died, and because she didn't have any relatives, nobody found the dead body for quite some time. It was the sound of Charlie's constant barking that eventually drew attention to the horror. Zeb told me all this, he said young Charlie had been in a bit of a state when he arrived at the kennels, terribly thin, and quite traumatized by the experience.

Zebedy is too old to run very far and me, well I am ok on a straight run, but the turns let me down every time. I am no good turning at all. Well I guess you all know that.

But Charlie, Oh boy can he run. He's up Falcon Reach in no time at all. That is the name of a high peak on one of our walks, so called because Falcons are supposed to nest there. I've never seen a Falcon's nest up there, not since I have been living at the kennels. Zeb says he's never seen a Falcon up on the Reach, and he's lived at Glenloyd for a long time.

"You seem to be settling in very well now Ben" said Peggy as we got back from our latest walk. I like Peggy, she has been very kind to me since I arrived a few weeks ago but there is a deep sadness in her eyes at times. I have been aware of this almost from the start of my being an inmate of Glynloyd Kennels.

It hadn't taken me long to discover for myself the reason for this unhappiness in the kennel maid. I had seen from the very first day the cruel treatment doled out to this girl by horrible Jake Binley. I had wondered why she stuck being treated in this way by the owner. I overheard her talking to Barry one day after a particular incident that had had Binley having another jibe at her. Peggy was in tears again, the young lad Barry trying to comfort her.

"I just love working at Glynloyd, Barry; it has been my life for so long; I know it isn't the same since Miss Whainwright died, and I suppose I must be thankful that Jake Binley kept me on when he bought the place. The thing is Barry, it means I can keep my eye on him, and make sure he doesn't hurt the dogs." I saw Peggy wipe her eyes. "He's a sly so and so Barry, just watch yourself."

So that was the reason the girl put up with so much torment from horrible Binley! It was to protect us dogs.

I had grown to love Peggy, well we all did. She is such a good hearted girl, and really kind to us dogs.

Jake on the other hand doesn't show us any kindness at all. Oh he's not cruel all the time, but he shouts a lot making some of the more timid dogs very frightened. We only get beaten on occasion. The monster carries a strap over his shoulder for that purpose. Zebedy, Charlie and I try to keep out of his way as much as we can.

It's Peggy we feel sorry for. Almost every time he sets eyes on the poor girl, we hear taunts of: "hello Tubby" or "hi Fat Chops" or he's pulling her pigtails. Why can't the bully leave her alone? We dogs feel upset when we know how hurt the poor girl gets from the constant treatment Binley dishes out to her.

Zebedy told me the other day, whilst we were out on our walk: "if I were a man, I would bif Binley in his fat guts! It might teach him a lesson." I knew Zeb and the rest of the dogs feel just like I do. Perhaps one day Binley will meet his match. I hope so.

Because we all felt the same about Peggy, we made a vow, to look out for the kennel maid. True we couldn't do much, but we promised to keep a close eye on her. We all mistrusted rotten Binley. We would do our best to help the girl, every way we could.

I suppose you could say that Zebedy was our leader. He was the eldest in the kennels, and the wisest. He had been my salvation when I first came to Glynloyd. Without him I don't think I would have lasted long. He showed me the ropes, comforted me when I cried for my mum in those first horrible days in the strange environment that was Glynloyd Kennels. The funny smells, the howling of other frightened dogs, the shear hell I found myself in. Zeb helped me through the first scary days, and I loved this gentle old boy for just being there. He was kind and very wise. He made our walks ever so interesting. He made the dark nights less frightening. I would always be in his debt.

But then one day out of the blue a terrible thing happened. Charlie, whose pen was just across the way from me, shouted over. "We seem to be a bit late going for our walk this morning Ben, I wish Peggy would hurry up, I'm busting for a wee." I agreed with Charlie, I was also crossing my legs. I hadn't been either since last night.

This wasn't like Peggy; she was usually here long before this time. We were soon to find out the devastating truth when a tearstained Peggy arrived at the pens. She came to my door, and in broken voice said. "Come on Ben boy, let's go and get Charlie, we will go for an extra long walk this morning."

Something was wrong! Why was Peggy so upset? We were soon to find out. As we went toward Zebedy's pen, we were surprised to see his door wide open. Something terrible must have happened. I felt sick. Was this the reason for the strange noises during the night? Bumping sounds so strange, and lots of loud whispers had woken me.

So it hadn't been a bad dream? Where was my friend, I wanted Zeb. Then I heard the answer. It was the voice of Jake Binley speaking words so awful that I just couldn't take them in. Binley was talking to a sobbing Barry. "The old boy died in his sleep during the night, he was taken away to be burned early this morning, you won't be seeing him again, so get used to it."

It was too much to bear. How could Binley be so hard about the death of such a nice old dog? Zebedy had been my best friend since I had been in Glynloyd Kennels. I could feel hot tears running down my face, "Oh Zeb how ever will I manage now, why did you have to die and leave me?"

I didn't feel like going for a walk now, and I don't suppose Charlie did but the call of nature was urgent, especially after such tragic news. We followed the weeping Peggy out of the kennels, and set off for a long sad walk.

We arrived back at the kennels to hear Binley telling the upset Barry to pull himself together and to get the pen cleaned out with disinfectant ready for a new arrival. "We are expecting another mutt shortly to fill the space that the old dog left so stop being such a baby; and get on with your work, otherwise you will be replaced by somebody who can do the job without bursting into tears every five minutes. Dogs die Barry get used to it."

I just couldn't believe anybody being so heartless but this was Jake Binley. He was as hard as nails and as rotten as they come.

Charlie and I carried on going for our walks with Peggy but it wasn't the same without Zeb. The old boy had left such a big hole in our lives at his passing. Peggy was upset as well. Zebedy had been such a special lad. You could say the old dog had been like a dad to the rest of the inmates of the kennels and it was pretty horrible without him but as they say, life has to go on. Well, life did go on, in a way that none of us could have expected for things were about to change in a big way, with the arrival of Boris: The IRISH WOLF- Hound...

To Lead Us Home

CHAPTER FOUR

BORIS

The following Saturday the new inmate put in an appearance. Charlie, in a hushed voice said: "Just look at him Ben, my, but he sure is a big un."

My friend sounded gob smacked. Now I am quite big, being a Border Collie and Charlie, well I suppose being a doggy mixture as I call him, isn't a bad size for his particular breed, (whatever that is). Charlie has a daft look on his face, and the kindest eyes but this Boris is something else. He is a giant of a dog, with a massive head, great big paws, and scruffy looking grey hair, with the longest legs I have seen in my entire life. He certainly looked down on myself and Charlie.

As time went on we were to realize, that Boris was as daft as a brush, not stupid, no certainly not stupid! However the huge dog was as crafty as a cart-load of monkeys. Boris knew exactly how to take care of himself. He soon settled into the pen Zebedy had occupied. It wasn't long before he was telling any other dog, who cared to listen, all about his life before coming to Glynloyd.

He always began in the same way, telling the tale with the marshmallow soft voice.
 "Yes my bonny boys; I belonged to an Old Irish Tinker by the name of Shanty Mulligan. I travelled the roads of old Ireland I did, for many a long year; I ran beside the caravan by day and slept under it by night. Mabel the carthorse was my companion as we went from village to hamlet down the leafy lanes of old Ireland, she pulling the caravan full of tinker's wares, me walking beside her."

"I loved the freedom boys, folks used to give us tit-bits. Mabel would enjoy a handful of hay or sometimes a sugar lump. Me well, I'd be partial to a taste of strong beer. Made me feel very jolly you know; or a chunk of bread and cheese. We visited quite a few of the orchards. Shanty Mulligan used to love his cider, many's the time he got so pie eyed with the drinking of the stuff that Mabel and I had to get us along the road whilst he slept it off. One particular place we stopped at on our travels was very special, the farmer's wife who lived there gave me a bowl of the best rabbit stew I have ever tasted."

With that the big dog drooled; at the same time licking his lip; as if the memory of the particular meal had reminded him of the happy event.

Then his mood seemed to change. Boris hung his great head and gave the biggest sigh I had ever heard.

"The reason I find myself in this predicament my bonny boys is that Shanty Mulligan went and died; yes died one night in his sleep, leaving Mabel and I to fend for ourselves. We walked around the lanes and streets for ages foraging for whatever food we could find, until some bloke caught me trying to pinch a chicken from his farmyard, and ran me off the place with a blast from his shotgun. The big dog gave another loud sigh.
"How I missed a bullet up the bum I will never know me bonny boys? All I do know is that it whistled noisily past my lughole, as close as a hair's breadth, I can tell you me lovely lads I was scared."

"When eventually people realized we were unaccompanied, after finding the corpse of Shanty Mulligan rotting in the caravan, the busy body authorities soon got into action.

Mabel was sent to a horse sanctuary for the duration of her life. As for me, well I could see the writing on the wall so I bolted just as fast as my legs would take me. I took care of myself for weeks, pinching the odd chicken, or picking some lovely morsel from a rubbish bin thrown away by some overindulgent human."

The great dog gave a sigh. "Some people don't know how lucky they are my bonny boys! Food and drink on tap. All taken for granted! Eventually the dogcatcher caught me, took two of 'em mind. I struggled like a dog possessed! They threw a net over my head, and locked me in the back of his prison van. They were too strong even for me!
"So here I am my bonny boys, Boris at your service."

With that this lump of a dog lay down on his belly, put his large head on his paws closed his eyes and went to sleep in the pen that up to a few days ago, had been occupied by my old friend Zebedy.

I feel sure Zeb would have liked this Irish comedian with his daft wit and warmth.
In a strange way his arrival at Glynloyd Kennels had helped Charlie and I to come to terms with the loss of our old pal.   We still missed him but as they say: life goes on.

It had also become apparent that Peggy loved Boris, and Boris loved Peggy. The big boy came on our walks with us, and we continued in this way enjoying the company of each other. It was also noticeable that Jake Binley had as little to do with Boris as possible. Between you and me, I think Binley is scared of our large friend. The owner of the kennels was however still hell bent on making Peggy's life as unhappy as possible. I for one could never understand why Binley treated her so, but then neither could anyone else.

Up till now Boris had kept his council. He watched and said nothing but things were about to change in a big way. Our lives in Glynloyd Kennels would never be the same again.

We had just come back from our morning walk and quite a walk it had been. Barry had accompanied us today. Binley had told Barry in front of us dogs that it was time he took on a more important role in Glynloyd Kennels. He must accompany Peggy on her walks. Trouble was, Barry is a bit slow. Not his fault, but he doesn't seem to see what's right in front of him.

We had reached the woods. Barry was holding the leads, all us dogs eager to be let free. I for one liked to pick my favourite spot to have a wee. This was always the practice once we reached the trees. However today things hadn't gone to plan. As we began our ramble into the woods, all of us pulling hard to get there, Barry took a tumble. He had caught his foot in a rabbit hole. As he fell he let go of the leads. As we took off for freedom, we heard Barry yell out in agony. He had hurt himself but I am afraid we did what dogs do, we carried on running. Charlie, with tongue hanging out at the side of his mouth, shouted over to me: "Just look at those daft sheep in the field over there, let's go and chase 'em". This remark brought me to my senses.

I stopped in my tracks. This wasn't right! I shouted as loud as I could.   "No Charlie, we are not chasing the sheep, it is very dangerous". Boris piped up, "No Charlie, Ben is right, we are not chasing our woolly friends. We don't want to get shot, I tried it once when I was on the run, the farmer almost had my guts for garters."

Just then Peggy called, "Ben, Boris, Charlie, come on the three of you, Barry is hurt. We have to get back to the kennels so with Peggy giving Barry a hand, we walked back to Glynloyd. After Peggy saw to the lad making sure he was bandaged and comfortable, Charlie, Boris and I had just been put back in our pens. Peggy was closing my gate when Binley came past.

"Hi fatty" he said while at the same time pulling one of her pigtails. He yanked it so hard and kept hold of it, still pulling on her hair, and Peggy yelled out in pain. "Why do you have to keep doing that Jake, I have just about had enough today, why can't you just let me do my job?" Tears of frustration and pain, once again filled her eyes.

Well, something snapped in me. I was out of my pen, with head down I charged at Jake Binley. I grabbed his arm and attempted to make him release the hold on the girl's hair. He let go of the pigtail and reaching for the strap he always carried on his shoulder, brought it down with such force across the front of my head. He yelled in temper at me. "You blasted mutt I warned you, this time you've had it. Perhaps now you'll learn who's the boss around here". Peggy screamed at Binley, and I saw stars.

As I crashed to the floor in agony I heard a thunderous bark coming from behind me. Boris had forced his way out of his locked pen. With a loud growl he came for Binley who in turn went charging and screaming along the passage between the pens. Shouting at the top of his wimpy voice "Help; somebody help", and to the charging Boris, "just you wait, I'll have you put down and fed to the pigs for this, see if I don't."

However, Binley was no match for Boris. His idle threats were wasted on the angry Wolf -Hound. From where I lay, dazed and bleeding from the wound inflicted on my head, I was able to witness a very valiant Boris open his mighty jaws and sink his teeth into Jake Binley's huge bum and shake him like a bit of rag!

The owner of the kennels was on the floor, screeching and yelling at the top of his voice, like the coward he is. "Get off me you lousy mutt," he said in a very wobbly frightened voice. You'll pay for this you lousy Irish swine."

Well, as luck had it, whilst all this mayhem was going on, a couple of people were visiting the kennels looking for a pet for their little boy. Fortunately they saw everything that had gone on, and were unhappy at the whole episode.

Well, events sure moved on after that. I supposed it must have been they who called the authorities.

Police inspectors came to Glynloyd asking Peggy lots of questions. The phone was madly ringing off the hook: newspaper reporters, wanting a good story. In fact, it was pure pandemonium.

The vet gave all of us dogs a check-up. I had three stitches in the wound to my head, Apparently I had been very lucky according to the vet who attended to me; it seemed an inch closer to me eye would have meant partial blindness. A few of us dogs were on the skinny side despite Peggy doing her best to feed us with what money she was allowed to spend on dog food.

Fortunately for one little dog there was a happy outcome. Minny, the tiny Terrier who had been living at Glynloyd since her elderly owner had died was taken by the couple that had witnessed Binley attacking Peggy and taking the strap to me, They had also witnessed the valiant Boris chase and catch the kennel owner, biting him on the bum for his punishment!

I overheard Peggy and Barry discussing the events. It seemed that Jake Binley had got his comeuppance. He was taken to court, and received a short prison sentence and was forbidden to keep dogs ever again, and it seemed that even the judge who took the case was seen to raise a smile when told of the Wolf-Hound's antics!

Glynloyd was closed down, Barry Jones was offered a job on Taffy Bryant's farm in the hills. Most of the other dogs had been found new homes. In fact, Peggy, Charlie, Boris and I were the only ones left.

Peggy Owen was a very different girl these days. I overheard her tell Barry Jones, before he left to take up his new job that a nice man by the name of Daniel Weaver had read in the newspaper all about the trouble at Glynloyd Kennels. It seemed that he, and his wife Victoria, had been friends of Pippa Whainright for years, and had in fact attended the auction after Miss Whainright had died. It appeared that Daniel Weaver had put in an offer for an old roll top desk he and his wife had always admired, which was accepted.

The most exciting thing of all was that Mr. & Mrs. Weaver had offered Peggy, Boris, Charlie and I a new home on their small-holding, somewhere called Apperley Grove East Yorkshire, whatever a small-holding was? I just hoped it would be big enough for all of us especially Boris!

So with great excitement, and packing everything in sight, we were off to our new life in Yorkshire, and Oh boy, what a life it was going to be!

To Lead Us Home

CHAPTER FIVE

A SURPRISE FOR ME

Apperley Grove was to be our new home; it was much bigger than Glynloyd. It was set in the lovely village of Skelby Dyke in East Yorkshire. There was a lovely feel about the place. It was fresh clean and homely. We hadn't been there very long when Boris said to me: "Oh Ben, Is this paradise or what, I reckon we've landed in Heaven me bonny boy?" I am pretty sure his Irish eyes were twinkling with joy. As for Charlie, he just seemed to be in a daze. I am sure this is the best home he has had, remembering the story he told me back at Glynloyd, as to how he had found himself in that awful place.

Apparently, he had come from somewhere called Rhyl, a Seaside place , on the coast of Wales. His master had been someone called a busker, who played a funny instrument he held in his hand and under his chin. Charlie said the noise made him cringe. He told me that he was used as a sympathy ploy by the old man to get people to part with their money and put it in the hat provided. However, Charlie said that one day the busker was beaten and robbed of his money and that was how a traumatized Charlie ended up at Glynloyd Kennels, so in a roundabout way, we had all come from sad beginnings.

As for Peggy, she seemed to be happy with the new conditions. She was to continue in the work as a kennel maid, the work she loved but now the conditions were more favourable to the ones we had left behind. Life at Apperley Grove was going to be wonderful for us all, even more so as far I was concerned, for unbeknown to me something pretty wonderful was about to take place at Apperley Grove,   something my wildest dreams couldn't have imagined.

We were met at the door of the large place by a homely looking lady. She smiled and shook hands with Peggy. "Nice to see you again my dear. It's a long journey isn't it love?" Peggy nodded her head in answer, agreeing with her new employer.
  "Come on in" said the kind, pretty lady. "The kettle's on, we can settle the dogs with a drink and then we can have a warming brew ourselves, and you can tell me everything that's happened in these past months since poor Pippa passed away."

Boris, Charlie, and I were taken to a warm comfortable place at the back of the building. I thought how nice it seemed after what we had come from. This place was nothing like Glynloyd. There was a lovely feeling about these kennels. I was shown into a lovely clean pen. "There you are Ben," said Victoria Weaver giving me a gentle pat. "Make yourself at home Lad." Then to the other two she said: "follow me boys, let's get you settled as well."

Boris and Charlie were taken to a pen each, just across from where I had been put. This was smashing. We were all together in this lovely place. Apperley Grove was to be our new home. This was more than I could have hoped for. Boris being the big lump he is, looked across to me from over the top of his pen. He called out in his Irish twang:
"What do you think of this me bonny boy? Heaven or what, I'm sure gonna like it here."   Charlie on the other hand hadn't said a word yet. He just sat there in his pen staring around with a daft look on his face.

I called across to him, "you ok Charlie?"   The doggy mixture nodded back to me, "fine Ben just fine".   Then from the next pen to me, came a voice I never thought I would ever hear again. I was in shock. This couldn't possibly be happening!

"Ben! Ben! Is that really you?" Over here, I'm over here." I turned to where the familiar voice was coming from. This just couldn't be taking place but it was. How did my sweetheart manage to be in this lovely place? With my heart almost jumping out of my chest I called back. "Nellie, My Nellie. Is that really you? How did you get here?" I was in an absolute daze of happiness. I never thought that I would see Nellie ever again. She had been sent away from Hilltop's a few months before me. This was simply amazing I could feel myself shaking.

I tried to put my nose through the grid of the front of my pen. Nellie was inches away from me. I needed to get to her side. How would I be able to tell Peggy and Victoria Weaver that Nellie and I must to be together? Somehow and I didn't know how I would have to let Peggy and Mrs. Weaver know just what Nellie and I meant to each other!

So I started to bark at the top of my voice, and I told Nellie to do the same. I told her also to run round in circles chasing her tail. She soon got the idea. With a glint of excitement I could detect from where I was, Nellie did as I suggested. We carried on like two demented idiots. Round and round in circles, barking and kicking up a storm.

Well I can tell you we caused a din. Boris and Charlie thought we had gone mad! When I was eventually able to explain to my two friends all about Nellie and I, they joined in the rattle.

Other Doggy Residents of Apperley Grove Kennels were in an uproar. Hearing the noise we were making, all the other inmates joined in the melee.

Victoria Weaver and Peggy must have thought we had gone mad. Both women came rushing into the pen area. Peggy came over to me. "Whatever is it Ben, this isn't like you at all?" I looked up at her. How could I tell her about my Nellie and I?

I began to jump up at the wall that separated my pen from Nellie's. I indicated to Nellie to do likewise. With that Peggy seeming to understand the urgency and opened my door. I quick as a flash, dashed through the opening, and began to jump up at my darling's door wagging my tail and wining as furiously as I could. Nellie at the other side was doing similarly.

Peggy and Victoria Weaver must have thought we had gone mad. Peggy grabbed me at the back of my neck. "Whatever is it Ben, Please boy, what's wrong?"
Then wonder of wonders. Victoria Weaver realized what all the fuss was about. She spoke excitedly to Peggy. "I think I know what this is all about girl, I will explain later. I'll let Nellie out of her pen, then we will see."

With that the clever lady opened Nellie's door. Nellie rushed towards the opening and straight to me. I was overwhelmed with joy. There was much whimpering, wining and rubbing necks. It was obvious to anyone who knows anything about love, that we were two very happy dogs. We had found each other after all this time. I never, in my wildest dreams thought that such a wonderful thing could happen. My Nellie was living at Apperley Grove Kennels and had been ever since she had left Hilltop's all those months ago.

The owner of Apperley Grove smiled at Peggy, "I was right Peggy, I was right". She then began to tell her new kennel maid the incredible story; and I listened as well.

It seemed that a very traumatized Nellie had arrived at Apperley Grove. She was supposed to be going to Glynloyd Kennels, like me, but according to Peggy, Gwyn Thomas my old master at Hilltop's, had rung Jake Binley to ask if he would give Nellie a home. However, Binley had refused to take her, saying that he didn't want any more bitches.

Victoria Weaver continued with the tale: "of course Daniel and I knew Glynloyd Kennels when Pippa owned them. They were run so beautifully then. Jake Binley worked there but only as foreman," and turning to Peggy said,

"I know Pippa was very fond of you my dear, I remember you on the few occasions Daniel and I visited, you always seemed to be enjoying looking after the dogs in your care, whereas Binley, on the other hand, appeared to be doing as little as possible". Victoria Weaver sighed deeply. "You know my dear, Pippa seemed to have a blind spot when it came to that fellow Binley. He used to sweet talk her, and she wouldn't hear a bad word said about the rogue but I wonder what she would think now, him getting his hands on Glynloyd and being sent to prison for cruelty to the dogs?"

I watched and listened to all this. I could certainly vouch for the fact that Binley could turn on the charm when it suited him.

This was all so fascinating. It answered a lot of questions. But for Nellie and I it was nothing short of a miracle. We had found each other again; we had a lot of catching up to do.

Victoria Weaver continued to fill Peggy in. "Well it so happened, that Gwyn Thomas rang us on the off chance, very strange really, it seemed he had been ringing round other kennels in the local vicinity with no luck, until someone gave him our number. After hearing Nellie's story we were only too happy to take her in. Daniel travelled to Hilltop's and brought her back here. Victoria Weaver paused for a moment. "Now I understand why we had such a job with the Labrador. She didn't want to leave Ben; it all makes perfect sense now."

"The poor dog was missing her companion. Just look at them both." Let's leave them together, they won't come to any harm."
Well I can tell you. That was wonderful. Nellie and I just sat and nuzzled each other in perfect happiness while Boris and Charlie, not really understanding the sequence of events looked on in amazement.

Next, in a whimsical voice, the kennel owner said "It' s funny how things work out for the best Peggy, pity we didn't have Ben at the same time as we had Nellie but somehow I think it was all mapped out. There is usually a reason for everything. Now the dogs are settled in their quarters with a drink, we can bring them some food in a little while. Let's go and get you settled in your own accommodation". With that both ladies left the pens.

I couldn't wait to introduce my two pals to Nellie. I knew they would just love her. The first thing Boris said to her was "what's the grub like here, can't wait to get stuck into a bowl of something meaty?" The Wolf-hound loved his belly. Charlie on the other hand just stood staring at Nellie. Between you and me I think Charlie fell a little in love with Nellie right from the first meeting. Didn't blame him mind, my Golden Labrador is a cracker, but she is mine.

Boris piped up again. "Yes me bonny boys, we have certainly fallen on our paws, just wish they would bring us some grub." Well we didn't have long to wait; we could smell the tripe, biscuits and beef before it got to the pens. The aroma was something else. Our meal eventually arrived on a trolley, being pushed by Peggy, who was accompanied by Victoria Weaver. The ladies were discussing the kennel maid's new accommodation. I was starving, I wanted my grub. I wasn't interested in rooms being cleared out, a rolltop desk that used to belong to Pippa Whainright, and wallpaper patterns, that was their terrain.

The food was eventually put onto the floor in enamel dishes. Mine was put down, with Nellie's, with reasonable portions put into each. Charlie's was about the same size as Nellie's and mine but I think Boris was more than pleased with the enormous portion he received. Of course, us being dogs we couldn't help but notice that Boris was given much more than us. It is in a dog's nature to be greedy you know. We can't really help it.

That didn't matter, Boris was a giant of a dog. He was given a very large bowl which was full to the brim with the delicious smelling food. With two or three mighty gulps Boris wolfed down the grub. He then licked his slobbery chops, lifted his great head, and looked lovingly at Peggy.

Boris was almost eye-level with the kennel maid. Peggy wasn't very tall, and the Irish Wolf- hound was very big. What happened next almost knocked Peggy off her feet. With his enormous tongue, Boris licked the kennel maid' s face. Peggy seemed startled for a moment. She smiled at the great fool, and gave him a big hug. "You are one soppy dog" she told the Wolf-hound, "but you are a very lovely fella." With that Boris seemed to swell even more in size. He lifted his left front paw and placed it gently on the kennel maid's shoulder. What a creep! Joking aside as I have already said, it was obvious that Boris loved Peggy and she loved him. I am not saying she didn't love the rest of us. She did, but Boris was her special guy.

The truth is, you can't help who you love can you? I loved my mum Floss and Belle, they were a million miles away from me now, and I knew I would never see either of them again. I had cried many tears for them. I knew I would always love them. However I have grown up a lot during these past months. I needed to. I just put the memory of Mum and Belle in a special place close to my heart, and moved on as best I could.
I had been fortunate to find my Nellie again. To me she was the best dog in the whole wide world. How wonderful was that?

Peggy and the owner left our pens chatting about how nice the room would look when the decorating and new furniture had been installed.

Of course this was nothing to do with us dogs. So Nellie, Boris, Charlie and I, with tummies nice and full, would just have to wait until it was time for our next walk. I cuddled up to Nellie. This to me was nothing short of Doggy Heaven.

CHAPTER SIX

THE ROLLTOP DESK

Victoria Weaver was showing the new kennel maid her quarters. Peggy looked around appraisingly. Yes, she was sure the rooms would be fine.

"I will ask Willie Ogden to clear out the two rooms: he's our odd job man",   Victoria said smiling at Peggy. "He's a funny old boy but he will do the job and get the rooms ready for you."

Just then Daniel Weaver poked his head round the door. "Oh there you are. Sorting out the rooms I see?" The co owner of Apperley Grove Kennels smiled at his new kennel maid. "When all the junk is moved, including the old rolltop desk, and the new carpets down, I think you will quite like them Lass. Both rooms have a lovely view across the fields to the coppice. Nellie especially seems to enjoy the walk amongst the trees."   Daniel smiled a broad smile once more towards Peggy. "She will like it even more now that she is back with Ben."

Daniel Weaver continued to talk to Peggy. "You must sort out which room you want for your sitting room and which for your bedroom. Both have an equally good view across to the woods and beyond, Nellie loves her walk amongst the trees, she will enjoy it even better now I am sure.   Before Willy begins work on the desk, I will ask him to bring you some furniture, it won't be new but I think you will find it is quite comfortable. The bathroom and kitchen you can share with Victoria and I, if that's ok."

Peggy thanked the Weavers. She was going to like working at Apperley Grove Kennels.
Daniel was about to leave, he turned at the door: "by the way Peggy, you won't have heard the latest news on

Jake Binley?" The girl shuddered at the sound of his name and shook her head.

The kennel owner continued. "It seems since all the trouble and his short term in prison, he was unable to return home. Reliable sources suggest that the fellow went to live in the Shetland isles, couldn't face people in his home town."

Peggy looked with relief at Daniel Weaver. "Oh thank you so much Mr. Weaver.
Good riddance to bad rubbish! None of us will have to set eyes on the horrible man ever again."

The kennel owner nodded his agreement and took his leave. Peggy Owen looked out of the window of the room she had decided would be her sitting room. She gazed out on the beautiful scene. A patchwork of green fields sloped down towards a large coppice. To the right was what appeared to be a stream, with woodland beyond. Peggy gave a sigh of contentment. Her new life in Yorkshire was going to be wonderful.

However before another thing was done, she must take the dogs for a long walk. She could decide on curtains and wallpaper later. The kennel maid walked towards the pens.

"Ben, Nellie, Boris, and Charlie, come on we must explore the area." Us excited dogs, on hearing Peggy, began to bark in unison. She opened each pen. "Come on, Nellie can show us the way". Nellie with an air of importance took the lead. In fact Nellie took the lead on every walk after that. True to what she had been told, the walk down to the coppice was indeed wonderful. Field after field, full of interest, especially for dogs! I liked the woods best. There were lots of rabbits with their white bob-tails, scurrying down holes in the ground, and those red bushy tailed things chasing up trees. Charlie is the best runner amongst the dogs. How he hasn't caught a rabbit yet I don't know!

Nellie soon made friends with Charlie and Boris. The latter made her smile a lot with his Irish blarney, twinkling eyes, and his wonderful gift of the gab. We thought at the time that nothing could better this but we didn't know what fate had in store for us.

Meanwhile back at the house, Willy Ogden scratched his head. "By gum, just when I thought I could take a break, they dump this lot on me" he said to nobody in particular.
Willy didn't reckon to work very hard if he could get away with it that is. He was a good sort, and he had a soft spot for Victoria Weaver. Willy had worked at Apperley Grove Kennels for years. The old boy reckoned he could turn his hand to just about anything. This included jobs such as laying carpets, wallpapering and carpentry.

Mr. & Mrs. Weaver had always been good bosses. When they asked Willy to clear out the two store rooms and get them ready for the new kennel maid, he hadn't really minded, especially when Daniel had slipped him a few extra bob in his pay packet. He couldn't turn that down! A few shillings would buy him an extra pint of his favourite beer. Willy loved his tipple, reckoned it gave him the vim and vigour to do some of the heavy work around the kennels. He was a Jack of all trades, and master of none, that was Willy Ogden!

He got started on the work. The old mangle was the first item to be moved out, followed by pictures, blankets, a couple of old tea chests, a load of ancient newspapers, and other bits of worthless rubbish. It seemed that Daniel Weaver had studied form, and had bet money on many a sure winner, but to Willie's knowledge, Daniel Weaver had never won a penny on horse racing!

Now it was the turn of the old rolltop desk. Willy took a deep breath, pulled his old corduroy trousers up round his middle, spit on his hands, rubbed them together and placing one hand each side of the old desk began to pull.

"By heck" he grumbled to himself. "This will take some shifting- the thing's as heavy as lead." Willy stopped to take a breather. He would be sixty-six years of age next birthday. He didn't like to admit as much, but it was true. He liked working for the Weavers! They were good bosses so it was important to show that he was up to every challenge, even when he felt anything but! He wasn't going to be put out to grass just yet. He gave another tug. Then another, eventually the solid desk began to move. Inch by inch the old boy managed to get the monstrosity out of the store room and into his large shed.

He remembered Victoria Weaver buying the 'thing' at an auction some time ago. 17th century they reckoned. It seemed that she and Daniel had always admired the old desk. It had belonged to a friend who had died. For the life in him Willy had never seen the attraction. To him the desk was just a heavy lump of oak. He had wondered idly whether they would like it as much if they had to shift the great lump about from room to room!

Willy mopped his sweating brow. He would sit down for a few minutes. Then he reckoned tackling the wallpapering and painting next would be in his best interest. The young lass had already told him that something floral and pink would be her choice for the paint and wallpaper, to decorate her rooms. After his rest he would go into town and collect the materials required for doing the job.

The hardware store was right next door to The Rose And Crown. This was the handyman's favourite Pub. Willy didn't know why he shouldn't take advantage of the situation. Besides after shifting the heavy desk, Willy reckoned he'd earned a pint of his favourite beer. He was very happy to be doing the job for the girl. Daniel had mentioned to him the reason for her and the dogs relocating from a place called Glynloyd Kennels. He didn't really understand much about what he had been told, but he liked the young Peggy, she was a good lass, and what about that great daft Boris? By gum, he was something else, and it was pretty obvious that Peggy really loved the dogs in her charge, especially the giant Irish Wolf-hound.

After buying the said materials to do the job, Willy got back in his old Morris Miner, and made his way back to Apperley Grove. He arrived back at the kennels. After a rest he would carry on with the rolltop desk. He reckoned the best thing to do with the thing, would be to strip off all the old varnish. So armed with everything required to do the job Willy began the work. The old boy puffed and panted- "By ek!" He muttered to himself. "This is going to take some elbow grease". Willy puffed and panted. This was a huge desk and Willy Ogden was short in stature and quite rotund, probably his habit of enjoying too much strong beer and his wife Edith's meat and potato pies didn't help when it came to doing a job such as this.

Willy battled on. Rub-rub with the oily rag and stripper, this was very hard work. He carried on for a further half-an hour, seemingly making little or no progress. He supposed that eventually the large piece of furniture began to look better. Next he thought he would tackle the inside but try as he may the rolltop wouldn't budge. Willy reckoned years of neglect and probably damp conditions had caused the rollers at each side of the desk to swell and harden.

The old handyman tried to lever his fingers underneath the opening of the rolltop but try as he might, the rolltop would not roll! Willy scratched his head; there must be a way to open the darn thing? He would take a break, make a mug of strong tea, eat his meat sandwiches and try to figure it out.

Willy remembered his dad using candle wax when he was having similar difficulties with a key that refused to turn in a lock or a rusted hinge on a door.
He would try that. Willy brought a candle from the drawer in his workbench. He lit the wick. As the candle melted the old man held it over the mechanism, at each side of the rolltop, at the same time trying to push the slats of wood that made the appendage move upwards. Suddenly with a creak and a groan the Rolltop began to slowly move upwards.

Willy heaved a sigh of relief- that had been hard work. He mopped his dripping brow- and continued to push the now more pliable desk-top until it was fully open.

The handy man stood back. Blimy he thought to himself, they believed in putting a load of drawers in the desks in them days? Fascinating! They don't make 'em like that now!

Willy thought that compared to the outside, which looked old and past its best, the inside was much cleaner, and more pristine. He put some beeswax on his cloth and began to rub along the inside of the old desk. As he did so- he touched a catch located just underneath the front lip. With great speed, a tiny drawer shot out at the front of the desk.

The sudden movement made Willy jump almost out of his skin. "Well I'll be blessed" he said to himself. "You can't see the drawer from the outside at all. Clever, very clever indeed!"   While the old man investigated the wonderful workmanship of the tiny drawers he saw something drop from the newly opened one. "What was that?"   Willy bent down and picked up a brown envelope. On the front in faded writing he read:

THE LAST WILL AND TESTAMENT OF MISS PHILLIPA WHAINWRIGHT.

CHAPTER SEVEN

THE WILL

Willy scratched his heads, "Well would you ever!"   The old boy turned the yellowing envelope in his hands. He reckoned this was a most important find so without much ado Willy thought he had better take the letter to his boss without delay.

The reaction he got from the Weavers was to be expected. Victoria Weaver especially seemed overawed with the discovery. Another person to be shocked and surprised was Peggy Owen.

Daniel Weaver took the old yellow envelope in his hand. He turned it over. He spoke to Victoria. "Just look at this love; I suppose we must take it to old Silas Butterfield. I will ring his office, and see what the solicitor has to say."

After a few moments of conversation Daniel put down the phone. He addressed his wife.
"Silas would like to see the document, he said to go to his office and he would take a look."

Things certainly moved on a pace after that. The next surprise to happen was to involve Peggy Owen. The poor girl was in a state of utter shock. She came into Nellie's and my pen. We didn't really understand what all the excitement was about, but we had noticed a lot of comings and goings recently concerning the owners and staff. We were soon to find out though!

"Oh Ben, Daniel says I have to attend a Will reading next week, a solicitor is coming here to see me, but why? It's nothing to do with me. I've never been to a Will reading!" Poor Peggy, She was so worried.

Apparently Willy Ogden had found this Will thing in an old desk. What did it mean, and why was Peggy so upset? Dogs know more than people think but none of us knew what a Will reading meant. Charlie said it sounded important. Nellie said, "Don't worry Ben, I don't think it's anything to do with us!" then Boris came up with a gem:

"Ah now, me bonny boys, I think someone called Will, wants to read something to Peggy!" I just hope it isn't something horrible."

Nellie and I listened to the other two dogs' interpretation of what they thought a Will reading was. None of us really knew what was upsetting our Peggy but we were to find out in due course. We didn't attend the 'Reading', after all it was nothing to do with us dogs. Anyway dogs aren't supposed to understand such things but as I have already said, dogs know more than people think. We just keep quiet about it, best that way. We just listen and learn; that is my philosophy. You gain dog-needed knowledge as you go along life's road if you stick to that truth. Admittedly there are some things we dogs aren't able to grasp, or be part of but that is the way of it.

THE READING

Silas Diggary Butterfield sat in the Drawing room talking to Daniel and Victoria Weaver. They were waiting for Peggy. Butterfield had been the Weaver solicitor for a number of years. So when the Will concerning Peggy had come to light, it seemed fitting that he should take care of this important document.

The plump red-faced solicitor took the Will from his briefcase, coughed loudly and taking a red spotted handkerchief from his pocket, blew his nose.

HERE IS THE LAST WILL AND TESTAMENT OF THE
LATE PHILLIPA WHAINRIGHT.

The old rolltop desk I leave to my friends Daniel &
Victoria Weaver, as I know they have always admired it.
I also leave them 7000 pounds, towards the upkeep of
Apperley Grove Kennels. The monies and rest of my
Estate totaling 28,000 pounds, I leave to my loyal
kennel maid and friend Miss Peggy Owen.

This then is my final Will and Testament.   Signed this
day. 20th 8 1953
Miss Phillipa Whainright.

Silas Diggary Butterfield smiled at Peggy, he had heard
in part what sort of life the girl had had whilst working for
the rogue Jake Binley. Well that so-and so was well and
truly out of the picture, and what's more he would
personally see to it that should the blaggard ever try to
get his foot back in through the door of Glynloyd
Kennels, rules would be put in place to stop him. The
solicitor closed the proceedings. Silas Diggary
Butterfield sighed deeply. This was what made his job
worthwhile.

When Peggy had taken in the full sense of what this gift
would mean to her, the girl knew what she must do! It
would take time, but that was fine. Glynloyd was in
need of repair, so while this was being done, she would
stay on at Apperley Grove but Peggy knew in her heart
of hearts that she must go home to Glynloyd.

The girl liked her work at Apperley Grove and she also
enjoyed her newly decorated rooms. Pink was her
favourite colour and Willy Ogden had done a wonderful
job. Everything was floral and pink. Peggy loved it, so
until such time as her own home Glynloyd Kennels was

ready she would enjoy the rest of her time with Ben, Nellie and the other dogs.

Good walks in the surrounding fields and woods were the order of the day. She would never forget the kindness shown by Victoria and Daniel Weaver but Peggy Owen knew she had her own destiny to fulfill.

When the day finally arrived Peggy Owen climbed into Daniel Weaver's car, accompanied by Boris and Charlie. She had decided that Nellie and I were happily together now, we had found each other! She would take our friends, Boris the Wolf- hound, and Charlie , the doggy mixture back to her own Glynloyd Kennels.

As I have already said Peggy really loved Boris, and she him. The soppy Wolf-hound had made a special friend of Charlie so it was fitting that Charlie was going back to Peggy Owen's kennels.

Peggy with tears in her eyes stroked my neck softly and gave me a cuddle. "I will miss you so much. Be a good Lad, I will never forget you Ben, never. Who knows we may meet again one fine day."

I just wanted to cry. Peggy had shown me the first bit of kindness when I arrived at Glynloyd. I loved the kennel maid so much. I knew with a hollow feeling in my tummy, that I would miss her as much as I had missed my mum and Belle in those early miserable days when I had had to leave Hilltop for Glynloyd.

I think Charlie was a bit overcome as well, he was happy to go with Peggy and Boris, but the doggy mixture had a soft spot for my Nellie, and he was going to miss her. I felt sure he would have a happy life at Glynloyd, and he would find he missed Nellie less and less as time went by for it was the way of things for us dogs.

Peggy Owen was a lovely person; she had been so good to me. Right from the first day at Glynloyd Kennels when I had arrived from Hilltop's Farm, alone and frightened, missing my Mum and Belle, she had comforted me. I would never forget the kind kennel maid nor would I ever forget my friends who were going with her. Perhaps we would all meet again one day?

It was rather a sad parting, for us dogs, but I'd overheard Daniel asking Peggy to visit and bring the dogs along. Perhaps it wouldn't be too bad, besides we dogs get used to partings! We have to! Thank goodness I had my Nellie but little did Nellie and I know that after Peggy and our friends had gone back to Glynloyd, we were to have the scare, and eventually the joy of our lives.

CHAPTER EIGHT

RYDER'S GROUND

Well the sad day for us dogs had arrived a lot faster than we wanted it to. Peggy was going home to her inheritance and taking Boris and Charlie with her.

The kennel maid had gone from unhappy put upon girl by her rotten and cruel self-appointed boss Jake Binley to owner of her own kennel, in a matter of a few weeks. She had hardly settled into her new rooms at Apperley Grove, and she was about to leave but Glynloyd was her true place, and I didn't blame Peggy for wanting to go home. She disserved to be happy after the years of torment dished out to her by evil Jake Binley. His troubles had certainly come home to roost. Nellie and I watched as Peggy disappeared out of sight. I was so glad that we were staying at Apperley Grove but it was a sad day nevertheless.

For quite a while Apperley Grove seemed rather quiet. We missed the daft Wolf-hound and Charlie, but life to us dogs is a series of missing pals and places.

Soon more dogs arrived. A soppy poodle called Missy, in for a short stay while her owner went on holiday to somewhere tropical. I only know this because I overheard Daniel Weaver saying to Willy Ogden, he wouldn't mind a few weeks at somewhere called The BAHAMAS! Whatever that meant? Two more dogs both looking rather traumatised, and badly in need of some TLC, also arrived at Apperley Grove Kennels. We were to find out that these two had been badly treated by their owner. They were used as punch bags by the drunken lout.

Their names were Prince and Rex, a couple of retired greyhounds, Rex told me that because they could no longer run and make money for their master, he and Prince had been almost starved to death. Had it not been for the intervention of a caring neighbour who had found them locked in an old barn on their owner's property, Rex reckoned they would have been dead. He remembered there were a lot of comings and goings on the property. People took photographs of the kennels where he had lived in squalor. There were big vans and lots of activity before the place was closed down.

Nellie and I reassured the two dogs that they had fallen on their paws and they would be fine here at Apperley Grove Kennels with Victoria and Daniel Weaver to take care of them. Nellie rather upset- asked me, " why do some people treat dogs so cruelly Ben?"
I couldn't give her a good answer.

Daniel Weaver came to the pens and with a cheerful voice said: "come on dogs it's down to me to take you for a walk from now on." Turning to me he said something that put fear into my heart.

"A couple of people are coming to see you Ben, they are friends of Victoria and I. They own a small-holding the other side of the Dales. They will be here later today."

Well I can tell you my heart sunk to my paws. What was going to happen now? I was happy here at Apperley Grove with my Nellie. All of a sudden, what had seemed a wonderful idyllic life here at Apperley Grove was to be turned upside down. What did these people from the Dales want to see me for?

I did my best to keep calm for Nellie's sake but I felt sick. I had been in situations like this most of my life and I was scared.

Nellie picking up on my anxiety asked - "What's wrong Ben?" I didn't want to upset her but I was very sad. The thought of leaving my newly-found happiness was too much to bear.

I cuddled up to Nellie. I loved her so. What was I going to do if these people wanted to take me away from Apperley Grove and Nellie? The thought was frightening. I couldn't lose her again.

Distant voices came nearer. I could recognize Daniel Weaver, but the other voice was from a stranger.

Daniel, accompanied by two other people came into the kennels. The man, an elderly gent peered into our pen. And with a warm voice said to me "By gum! You're a good looking fella"

Turning to Daniel. "We've been looking for a Collie for a while. My but he's a beauty! About twelve months old you say give or take a month or two?"

Daniel answered the man. "We've had him for a few weeks George - came to us from North Wales with a couple of other dogs. The place was temporarily shut down because of the then owner's bad reputation for cruelty. The man turned to the lady with him. "What do you think of the Collie Gert, shall we take him?" I looked from Daniel, to the elderly couple. This was a nightmare.

The lady answered. "Oh George, I think the dog's lovely just look at his curly black and white coat, he's a bobby dazzler and no mistake. A bit thin mind, and all arms and legs- but we can soon fatten him up, and what about those gentle eyes George, have you ever seen such beautiful eyes?"

All this flattery might have gone down well with some, but for me it was too much.
I was just a dog, and I wanted to stay here with Nellie. By this time Nellie was getting the idea. She could see what was going on as well as me. There was a strong possibility that we would be parted again.

I could feel Nellie begin to tremble, so I snuggled closer to her. They wouldn't take me without a fight. So I told her not to worry, I would sort it. I began to bark as ferociously as I could and at the same time I began to limp! If I frightened the old couple and made them think I was lame perhaps they would think twice so I carried on until my throat felt sore. I also bared my teeth. That would show them!

Daniel Weaver rushed into our pen. He was surprised as well at this out of character behaviour. Another person surprised by my outburst was Victoria Weaver. Neither she nor Daniel had heard me explode like this.

The elderly lady quite taken aback by my outburst asked Daniel what was wrong with me, and what was wrong with my leg and why was the Labrador so upset?

Daniel patted me. "Quiet down boy, leave this to me." With that he left our pen and I heard him begin to tell the Marshalls all about Nellie and I and the life we had had right the way back to Hilltop's farm.

The couple listened to Daniel with much interest. The lady looked towards Nellie and I and with a tear in her eye she said: "no wonder you were so upset boy, you didn't want to be parted from your girl again did you, well never mind boy that isn't going to happen."

Well it turned out that Mr. & Mrs Marshall decided that they would take both Nellie and I to their small-holding, (whatever that was). Apparently Daniel's explanation and my outburst had worked.

So with much relief on mine, and Nellie's part, that we would be staying together after all, there was a warm goodbye to The Weavers, with a promise to keep in touch. Nellie and I were off to Ryder's Ground in somewhere called The East Coast of Yorkshire.

Nellie and I were put in the back of an old pick-up truck along with the papers about us: vet treatment and so on and information about where we came from. Also included were the few items that belonged to us. These comprised of a couple of blankets and a water bowl. Nellie had a very chewed up old soft toy. She was allowed to take that as well. I think it probably started life as a teddy bear. As Nellie had chewed off both its ears and half its face, (this was before I came on the scene) it could have been anything? I suppose you could say the soft toy had given her comfort.

With a cough and a splutter, the car began to move. Nellie and I sat on the back seat and watched as we drove away from Apperley Grove Kennels. Victoria, with a handkerchief held to her eyes, waved a watery farewell. Daniel also looking rather sad as he bid us goodbye.

The old car gathered speed. We were soon travelling towards our new home. Nellie snuggled closer to me. I sensed that she was feeling as apprehensive as I was. What was a small-holding? How far were we going?

Well it turned out that Ryder's Ground was only a few miles away from Apperley Grove. It was situated on the Coast at Churchly-on Sea, between Whitby and Smugglers' Keep. I knew this because I kept my eyes and ears open. As I told you earlier, dogs know far more than people think. It's just that sometimes it pays to act dumb!

It was to turn out that we would see Victoria and Daniel quite regularly for it appeared that Daniel and George Marshall played skittles for the local pub, The Seafarers' Rest. Victoria and Gertrude Marshall would spend time together at Ryder's Ground preparing a meal for when the skittles match was over so the two couples would easily keep in touch. Nellie and I would see Victoria and Daniel Weaver from time to time so to us that was a comfort.

We arrived at Ryder's Ground about mid morning. The car stopped. George Marshall opened the door, and peering into the back said: "come on you two, let's be 'aving you, Gert will show you your new home."

Nellie and I climbed down from the uncomfortable back seat, and into a yard to be met by the strangest noise I had ever heard. Nellie slunk a little closer to me. "Whatever is that Ben?" Well I couldn't answer her because I didn't know! All I was aware of though was that this Ryder's Ground place seemed a queer set up, quite the strangest place I had ever been in.

Still the strange noise continued. "HE HAW, HE HAW. " Nellie got behind me. She was really scared.

George Marshall, seeing the fear in Nellie and I, (she was more scared than me) said,
"come on you two, meet Dunk the Donkey. He won't hurt you, just as long as you remember not to let him get

behind you." Why did Mr. Marshall laugh when he said that? Just then Gertrude Marshall came to Nellie and I, and patting us both said. "Dunk is pretty harmless, although he does have a few cheeky tricks. He is very noisy, likes the sound of his own voice. Come on you pair let me introduce you to him, after all you will be living here from now on."

We followed Mrs Marshall to where the noise was coming from. There was a small field, fenced in luckily for us! Beyond that there was what looked like a barn. I knew what a barn was, I had spent many happy times in one with my mum. Belle and Nellie back on Hilltop's. I sighed. Hilltop's seemed a million miles away but at least Nellie and I were back together.

"HE HAW, HE HAW". There it was again. Then we saw where the noise was coming from. Well I had seen Carthorse on Hilltop's, but this was the first time I had seen a donkey and a daft looking donkey at that. Nellie transfixed said "look at the size of his ears Ben, is that normal and what about those yellow teeth?" As we stared at the donkey, he sort of rolled his lip away from those big teeth, and appeared to be laughing at Nellie and I showing us his pink gums as well as his horrible yellow teeth.

Gertrude Marshall walked towards Dunk. What a silly name! She proceeded to rub his nose, whilst talking softly to him. I was to learn to my cost at a later date why the donkey was named Dunk.

"Now come on you two, I've got work to do" Mr. Marshall was carrying our belongings in his arms. "Let's get you settled in the barn, then I'd like to show you both round the place." Turning to his wife, he said, "come on lass, I could do with a cup of your strong tea before I do anything else. My throat is parched. While you put the kettle on I'll settle the dogs."

Nellie and I were taken across the large yard. Dunk was still shouting his silly head off but we could also hear another unfamiliar sound. As we walked with George Marshall, the sound became louder and louder.

Our new owner, probably noting that we were worried, well Nellie was, called out to where the sound was coming from.

"Now that's quite enough Lavender you noisy Goat, be quiet." George Marshall took us towards this goat. "Meet Nellie and Ben, they have come to live with us, now behave yourself and be nice."

Thank goodness the Goat was in a secure area, I didn't like the look of her, and by the way she was staring at Nellie and I, the feeling was mutual. Her slit-eyed stare spoke of dislike, and despite what George had said I don't think 'nice' was in her makeup.

Well that was two animals I didn't think were going to be friends. I wasn't as sure now, that the move to Ryder's Ground was going to be such a good idea after all. George Marshall must have noted Nellie's and my ongoing discomfort at being introduced to the couple of animals with attitude, and steered us away towards a small barn. He opened the doors. "Come on inside, this will be your new home. It's nice and warm in the winter, and cool in summer". As we stood and looked around the place, I was taken back to the barn at Hilltop's where I spent my early months with my mum, Nellie and Belle. Perhaps it wasn't going to be so bad after all.

Our new owner put the blankets down on the sweet smelling hay piled at the back of the building partially covered by a wooden trellis. This was so much like Hilltop's that for a moment I was back in that never to be forgotten home of love. I half expected my mum to be sitting waiting for me.

Nellie brought me back to the moment. "This is lovely Ben, perhaps it won't be too bad when we get used to things, and who knows we may be able to make friends with the resident animals, after all we are nice dogs!" I just looked at Nellie. She was lovely and so trusting! I suppose it would be a good idea to make friends with these Ryder's Ground residents! After all we would be living here from now on. Well I hoped so anyway!

Mrs Marshall picked up our blankets that a while ago her husband had put on the sweet hay. She spread them out again further into the corner. "You will be better there, well out of any draught, the wind can be keen in the winter we are rather high up at Ryder's Ground." George Marshall looking on, said, "you are an old fusspot missus, the dogs would have been fine where I'd put the blankets."

The old man smiled and looking towards Nellie and I he said in a teasing way "women, what can you do with 'em? He continued "by the way, the two animals you saw, Dunk and Lavender usually share the same field but Dunk has been up to his tricks just lately so we put the goat on her own for a while, but they will be back together very soon, and as a reminder don't forget what I told you about not turning your backs on Dunk."

Nellie and I sniffed around the sweet hay; this was a nice barn, as barns go. Mr. & Mrs Marshall were good people, so all things considered I didn't think it would be too bad living at Ryder's Ground despite Dunk the Donkey and Lavender the Goat although there seemed to be a mystery concerning the donkey.

We were to meet more animals later, including a few sheep, I hoped George had been told about my difficulty with these woolly animals. It turned out that my new owner had already been put in the picture. It seemed he wasn't bothered about having a sheep dog. As it seemed he could manage these few sheep himself. Apparently Gertrude had just fallen in love with me anyway, that was the main reason for them having me.

Firstly, we got stuck into a bowl of food that Gertrude Marshall had just put in front of us along with a welcome drink of water.

After a good night's sleep, Nellie and I were awakened by another raucous rattle.
"Cockadoodledo", and again "Cockadoodledo". Nellie, still half asleep said in a concerned voice: "what was that Ben?" I couldn't answer. It was another noise unfamiliar to me but I tried to allay any fears by telling her it was just another Ryder's Ground specialty! Claud the cockerel certainly turned out to be a proper show off alright, strutting around the place, in front of all the chickens. They thought he was something but to me he was just a squawking big-headed twit.

George Marshall called us. "Come on dogs time for a long walk, I'll get you used to the area, and introduce you to a few more inmates. We have quite a selection one way and another. Take no notice of Claud he likes the sound of his own voice, he's a good cockerel a bit of a show off though". George Marshall smiled that smile that we were to learn meant that there was another animal to be careful of.

Nellie and I rushed out of the cosy barn. We wanted to show our new owners that we were obedient dogs, well it pays to keep on the right side of the people who are taking care of you! Nellie and I had had too many changes in our young lives. We needed to know that we belonged here permanently. For despite the donkey the goat, the cockerel, and Hector the big fat goose, we reckoned that living at Ryder's Ground with the Marshalls was going to be ok.

The Yorkshire Countryside is magic, miles and miles of open fields, woods to explore, and rabbits to chase. These fluffy animals are too fast for me, well especially with my bad leg! Anyway, no need to chase them any more, not with the good grub put in front of Nellie and I!

Nellie looks ever so well and we are both happy. We regularly meet other dogs whilst out on our walks including Cassidy, the Old English sheep dog, (I wish he wouldn't keep calling me Benny) my name is Ben. I am proud of my name. I believe Belle gave me the name back at Hilltop's.

Nellie and I often talk about my mum Floss and Belle. It seems a life-time away since I felt Belle's arm around my neck as she pleaded with Gwyn her dad not to let me go. I wish I could tell her that I'm happy, and Nellie and I are together and living at Ryder's Ground.

Spider is another rescue dog, I heard his Master, by the name of Andrew Beamish telling George what a sorry state he had found the Greyhound in. It seemed that Spider had been chucked out on the streets when he could no longer win races and make money for his owner. He told George that he had taken the greyhound to be company for Cassidy.

Sounds like another horrible beggar. Nellie said it reminded her of the story I told her about Jake Binley! Well he was one person I would rather forget. He had got his comeuppance. Served him right, I was often to recall the time Boris bit Binley on the bum. That had been very satisfying to me.

Andrew Beamish seemed nice. Cassidy and Spider have a good master in him especially as he is the local butcher, no wonder he's as fat as lard. With red hair and beard, he looks funny. When he and George are sharing a joke, his fat belly wobbles up and down. It always makes Nellie and I laugh (dogs can laugh you know.)

So this then is how our walks proceed. The two men chat and chuckle with each other whilst us dogs, enjoy each other's company. We dogs chat amongst ourselves, explore the woods and fields, chase the funny red things with bushy tails up the trees, have a few good wees, chew a stick or two and enjoy an occasional drink in the stream that runs through the wood. Life sure was good here at Ryder's Ground.

Eventually Dunk the donkey and Lavender the goat were reunited. We found out from the goat that Dunk had knocked her over, with his too heavy prodding. I was to experience something similar, when I did what George had told me not to do and let the donkey get behind me!

Hector the goose is another force to be reckoned with. He is nasty! A great wobbling tub of goose grease! One day he really was to get his just deserts, and oh boy did I enjoy it when that day came."

Time went on a pace, and when Nellie and I had been at Ryder's Ground for
a few months Gertrude suggested to George that we go to the Seaside, whatever that was?

"Come on George, the dogs would love it, it's almost autumn, the nights are drawing in, it will soon be too dark and cold."

We had just got back from our walk. George answered his wife. "Don't know love, we can't leave the animals for too long" Gertrude with a pleading voice said, "we could ask old Harry Potts to keep a weather eye on the place. He's a good sort, offer him a couple of pints, you know he likes a drink. Besides we need a break before winter sets in."

I had no idea what seaside meant, but it must be good if Gertrude Marshall wanted to take Nellie and I. It would be nice to get away from noisy Claud the cockerel. He was such a show off. Mind you there wasn't much to choose between Hector the goose and Claud, when it came to showing off.

Eventually Gertrude got her own way, George phoned Harry Potts, the answer was 'yes', he would be happy to oblige, for a couple of drinks at The Seafarers' Rest. So with no further ado the following morning found Nellie and I seated in the back of the old car, along with our blankets and a basket full of things required for a day at the Seaside.

We were soon driving away from familiar surroundings, over fields and hills, down bumpy lanes. After what seemed ages, we began to notice something different! There was a strange noise and an unfamiliar smell. Nellie, sounding worried said; "What's that noise Ben, I don't like it?" I tried to reassure her. "It's ok Nell. Don't worry." However, truth to tell I wasn't keen on the funny smell or the noise, either. Eventually the car stopped. George opened the back door and peered inside. "Come on you two, we've arrived."

I looked in amazement at what was before me. Where had the grass gone? And what was that? I was looking at the biggest duck pond I had seen in my entire life. It went right down to the bottom of the sky.

Gertrude came round the back of the car. "Come on jump out we've arrived."
I was first out. I thought it best due to the strange looking ground. Well let me tell you this was pretty queer! As I jumped and landed, my paws slipped into the soft stuff. Nellie followed closely. She landed with a thud.

"Help Ben" she cried. "My paws have gone into the powder! I can't see my paws." George; noting the panic said to the dogs: "don't look so worried you daft pair. It's what they call 'sand' ". George sat down on the stuff, and began to take his shoes and socks off. "This is the Seaside", and pointing with his finger towards the end of the big duck pond, "and that over there is 'the sea'". Meanwhile Gertrude started to take her shoes and stockings off. "I'm going for a paddle George! The salt water will do my bunions good."

I looked at Nellie who was just standing in the stuff and seemed to be sinking. I gazed about me. There were other dogs that seemed to be enjoying the soft powder. Gertrude called us to follow her. This was something very funny but after a while I began to feel that it couldn't be a bad thing, after all, the other dogs seemed to be enjoying the experience. As for George and Gertrude, they were having a smashing time.

So I said to Nellie, "Come on Nell; I don't think this seaside thing will hurt us". She sort of wriggled free and we both followed our owner to the massive duck pond.

Well, let me tell you. Nellie and I had the best time ever. The big duck pond was smashing so whilst Gertrude paddled her 'bunions' Nellie and I splashed and played in the water. It was very different from anything else we had experienced. We ran from the soft stuff into the water, then back again.

It was lovely to see my sweetheart so happy. I don't think I have ever seen her so excited. Her tongue was hanging out and her mouth was wide open. However, I think she did a little too much though for later on she seemed to need a very long rest.

Gertrude and George appeared a bit concerned about the length of time Nellie spent resting as well. I overheard them talking as they packed the blankets and other stuff back in the car. When I asked Nellie if she was alright- she told me not to fuss but to tell the truth, I was worried that Nellie may have overdone it at the seaside.

A few days after our trip to the seaside, Mr. Price the vet was called. He came into our barn and examined Nellie. To tell the truth I had become rather worried. Nellie was different somehow. She seemed to want to spend time on her own and another thing, I noticed My Nellie was getting rather fat! It wasn't like her at all she didn't want to play either.

After the examination was over. Mr. Price turned to my owner who was looking on.
"You were quite right George. The Labrador is pregnant. About five weeks I would say. She will probably give birth to two, or perhaps three pups in a short space of time. Just keep an eye on her but she will be fine."

Now I was really worried, what was "Pregnant" and why did my Nellie have to have it? She had been touchy and snappy ever since our trip to the seaside. Wish we hadn't gone now if this pregnant change in her was the result.

The next few days were a bit miserable for me. Nellie didn't seem interested in anything. Even our walks in the fields and woods were too much for her. Did this pregnant thing mean fat because my Nellie was very round in her tummy area. No wonder she didn't want to go for a walk anymore!

Another thing that upset me was the fact that Nellie didn't want me round her. I hated this change in her. It wasn't like my gentle Nellie at all.

I was really fed up so after my walks I tried to find something in the yard to occupy my time. Gertrude and George made regular checks on Nellie, who by now was spending more and more time in the barn. Gertrude kept telling me not to worry, and that one day very soon I would get a lovely surprise!

To be fair Nellie had tried to reassure me that everything would be ok but I wasn't convinced. Besides, I didn't want a surprise. I just wanted my Nellie back to how she was, before the seaside trip had caused such a change in her, a change, that had made her fat and moody, and taken away my own happiness.

The weeks moved on a pace. Then one night in the early hours there was such a panic. Nellie had been moaning for some time. I was worried sick so I started barking trying to attract the attention of my owners. Gertrude and George had rushed to the barn in their night-clothes. Mr. Price the vet was called, I couldn't stand to see my Nellie like this. How I blamed the visit to the seaside a few weeks ago. Nellie had been fine until then.

But now to see her in this state really upset me. I tried to get close to Nellie, what could I do to help her? She was in great pain, and I felt useless. Suddenly there was a gut- wrenching yell from Nellie. I felt sick. Nellie was dying and I couldn't help her.

After what seemed like ages of serious activity around Nellie, hot water being called for by the bucket full, and towels being used a lot:

"There girl, good girl, it's all over." It was Gertrude Marshall. What did she mean, "It's all over?" I tried my best to get to my Nellie, but there were legs all over the place. Mr. Price was kneeling down over Nellie. Gertrude looked to be crying into her pinny. I had never seen such anxious activity around Nellie. Something was very wrong. All the time people were telling me to go away! I was getting very confused.

George took hold of my collar and patted me gently on my head. "Come on boy, this is women's work! Let's go for a walk, there's nothing we can do here". As we left the barn I heard another noise that scared me out of a year's growth, a sort of squeaking, and snuffling sound. I didn't like it! These funny noises were coming from where Nellie was lying. This was awful. I felt sick.

I followed George out of the barn but every instinct in me wanted to stay with my Nellie. Perhaps she was ill or at worst dead? I could feel my legs trembling. My lovely life had turned into a nightmare.

George patted my neck. "It's alright boy; don't look like that. Nellie will be just fine". We walked around the yard, past Dunk and Lavender. Dunk shouted his usual

"He ha" and stared at me with that, I'll get you look but I wasn't in any mood to play his daft games. One day! Oh yes one day!

The next thing to happen almost made me jump out of my skin. It was Gertrude running across the yard beckoning furiously with her hand. "Come on you two; come and see Nellie's puppies, they are so beautiful."

What did she mean Nellie's Puppies?

George gathering speed ran towards the barn. I followed not knowing what we were going to see. I walked slowly towards the sweet hay. The first thing to hit me was a different smell, sort of warm and sickly. I then heard a strange noise coming from where Nellie was lying.

Nellie lifted her head and looked at me. I took a deep breath. My Nellie wasn't dead after all!   She was alive! But she seemed different somehow, softer and more grown up. She spoke words I didn't understand.

CHAPTER NINE

EVIE AND ZEBEDY

"Come and meet your puppies Ben." I went closer. There was that snuffling noise I had heard earlier. Then I saw them! Two squeaking wet little things and they were eating my Nellie's tummy! As I looked at the scene before me, I didn't understand what was going on. Why did Nellie have to get them, these funny little wet squirming creatures who were snuffling and biting her and making a funny noise?". All of a sudden I felt lost. I didn't understand any of this, who were these new snuffling creatures? I didn't think for one moment I would like them, ever! Why did my Nellie have to get them?

However, I was soon to change my opinion on the situation. Our puppies soon became tubby little bundles of joy, very soon wrapping themselves completely around my own heart. Little Evie, gentle, just like her mother, is a mixture of golden and brown fur, and has a stubby tail with a white flash on the tip. She is a lovely little darling.

Zebedy on the other hand is a little monkey, full of mischief, and into everything. "Quick-solver" George calls him. He may have his mother's angelic face, but anything less like an angel you won't find! Mind you, Zebedy is very handsome indeed. He follows me! He has a black and white thick curly coat, and a white bib. He has a look of my mum Floss. I was pleased about this. I knew my mum would love these two pups. It was unfortunate that she would never know about Evie and Zebedy but that was the way of things. I had to accept that fact.

Little did I know at that time what was around the corner! It isn't always correct to assume things before they happen. Surprises do sometimes take place when you least expect them to.

Nellie is a wonderful mum but I know she gets tired. These two are a handful.
They are into everything. The pups get bigger every day. They are about five months now. Evie is the smallest, her nature is lovely. She has her mother's colouring, a bit darker than Nellie and the white tip on her stubby tail is so cute.

We have to watch them all the time with the other residents of Ryder's Ground, not so much Evie, she usually stays round her mother, but Zebedy is something else. He likes nothing better than tormenting Lavender the goat, and Hector the goose. One day it would become apparent to the young pup, that he had bitten off more than he could chew, and it served the little monkey right.

Nellie called me. "Oh Ben! He's at it again, will you go and get him away from the duck pond?" I answered "ok Nell leave it to me." I walked over to the pond, for the fortieth time, and in my sternest voice shouted "ZEBEDY! For the last time, will you come away from the pond. If Hector bites you, it's no use you coming to me or your mother! It will serve you right." I turned away, and chuckled to myself. My son was a live wire there was no mistaking that fact but unless I made him toe the line he would be a handful.

The pup watched his dad walk away. He followed a little way behind. Under his breath, the pup muttered. "Ah, but you didn't say anything about the hens did you Dad?"

As Ben went back into the barn, to assure Nellie that he had warned their son that the duck pond was out of bounds from now on, Zebedy slinked off, towards the hen run.

As he came round the corner of the cornfield Zebedy thought the best way to handle the surprise attack was to creep as quietly as he could until he was almost on top of the hen house. At this time of day most of the hens would be resting on their perches. Zeb got down on his belly. The daft hens certainly wouldn't be expecting a visit from him.

As he crawled slowly towards his target, He came face to face with Claud the one eyed bad tempered Cockerel. Claud had lost his eye ages ago in an accident with a garden fork, it had been his habit to watch for hapless worms George unearthed whilst digging potatoes. The cockerel was quite tame and it amused George and Gertrude to watch Claud's skill at catching the occasional worm. Unfortunately for the greedy bird he stuck his head down to the dirt just as George was sticking the fork in! There was an almighty squawking as the fork made contact with Claud's left eye. Zebedy remembered hearing his mum and dad discussing the accident at the time. All the young pup knew was that Claud was one very bad tempered bird ever since that unfortunate happening. It would be fun to torment him.

Claud,with his sharp claws, scratched the ground in anger, feathers flying, and a blood-curdling screech came from his open beak. He headed straight for the pup. Nobody messed with him or his girls. Besides it was time this young monkey was taught a lesson. The one eyed bird had had enough of Zebedy and his tricks.

As he charged, full pelt towards the naughty pup, intending to give him a nasty peck, Zebedy backed off, straight into the hen house. With more squawks from the startled hens as they stumbled and fell about, the pup, felt that after all that, this hadn't been such a good idea, charging at the escaping and startled hens. However, he couldn't be seen to back down now!! The furore coming from the hen house was enough to send alarm bells ringing not only at Ryder's Ground, but possibly, as far off as old Harry Potts' place!

George arrived on the scene, puffing and panting, to be confronted by utter mayhem. In as angry voice as he could muster he said:

"Zebedy you young scoundrel. What in the blazes are you doing now?" He looked around him at the frightened hens, some with missing feathers, others looking glassy eyed and traumatised. "Do you want to give me a heart attack? Just look at the mess you've caused, what on earth do you think you are doing?"

As George carried on the angry tirade, Gertrude, worried at the noise, came huffing and puffing, and arrived at the battered hen house. By now George had got Zebedy firmly held by the scruff of his neck.

He looked at his wife. "What are we going to do with this young devil Gert?"
"We can't have this all the time. He's a young monkey. I am going to have to think what to do for the best" By this time, Nellie and I were on the scene. If I had told Zebedy once, I had told him a dozen times to leave the hens alone. Now I could see that George was really angry and I didn't blame him. Zeb had gone too far this time.

As we watched the angry George put our pup in the barn and shut the door, we wondered whether this was it, as far as Zeb was concerned.

By this time, Nellie was in tears. "Why can't he behave himself Ben, like Evie, she isn't a bit of trouble. Zebedy will be the death of me." I shook my head. "Don't know Nell, wish I did. Try not to get too upset love; hopefully the little devil will grow out of his naughtiness before very much longer."

Zebedy was shut in the barn for about two hours. We could hear him whining, and it upset his mother, but he had to be taught a lesson. The trouble was, Zeb seemed totally uninterested in behaving himself for more than a couple of days. He had so much energy that nothing short of locking him up would stop his antics.

George finally calmed down enough to let Zebedy join his Mother, his sister Evie and I back in our own barn.

Evie and Zeb played nicely together for a little while. We thought the punishment of George locking our son in the big barn for a few hours had done the trick but how wrong could we be!

We had all been on our usual morning walk with Gertrude. She took us to some interesting places. We especially liked Bluebell Wood; it was our favourite. I now enjoyed chasing, and eventually catching a rabbit. Nellie doesn't like me catching rabbits, she thinks it's cruel, but I am a dog, and it's what we do! Mind you I can't say I like to eat them, the fur gets stuck in my throat. Over time, I had learned, how to catch a rabbit or two, finally realising that it was quite a good sport. It's a dog thing you know!

We had been back from our walk for about an hour. Nell and I were resting when all of a sudden, there was an almighty bang! I rushed out into the yard, to find Zebedy closely followed by Evie running round the yard with Gert's washing line full of wet and now dirty clothes wrapped around their necks.

The bang we had heard was the clothes post being uprooted by the two pups.

Well this was it. Apparently. Evie seeing her brother up to his usual tricks, and worrying what the punishment would be for him this time, had tried unsuccessfully to stop him pulling on the wet clothes. Although it would appear that both pups were equally guilty in the act of willfully ruining the clothes on the washing line, it would turn out that once again it was Zeb who had gone against authority. This young rascal was in for the shock of his life.

To say I had never seen Gertrude in such a bad temper as the one she was displaying at the moment would be an under-statement. With a face as black as thunder she charged at Zebedy with a broom, shouting and screeching at the top of her voice!

"You young monkey, wait till I catch you, just look at my nice clean washing." She stopped to get her breath. Then came another outburst!

"Well I say clean, but it's absolutely filthy now you have wiped it all over the mud, just look at my white table cloth and sheets! As for George's vest and pants, they are ruined absolutely ruined." Gertrude thought she wouldn't mention her own under garments. That would be too embarrassing.

After retrieving the said washing, Gertrude put them in the kitchen sink to scrub before putting them back in the wash-tub for a second wash. Of course, I knew that Gertrude Marshall's bark was worse than her bite, but all the same the pups had gone too far this time. My little Evie, being dragged into her brother's antics, because she was trying to stop him was hard to swallow. I suppose I hoped against hope that this time Zeb would learn a valuable lesson: every action has a consequence. The quicker he learned that truth, the better it would be!

Zebedy was once again put in the big barn, along with his sister this time. Now Nellie and I were very upset, both pups locked away, and Evie especially not deserving of this punishment. I was very angry now, how could Zebedy be so defiant, the young monkey, and to get his gentle sister into trouble was too much to bear.

Well after that performance, I was determined to bring Zebedy down to earth with a very loud bump! How could he treat his mother and I in such a way, and as for his little sister, this was definitely the last straw?

Nellie and I tried to stay out of the way as much as we could. I suppose I felt responsible for my pups' actions. I don't know why though! Nellie and I had tried to teach our young imps right from wrong but some lessons are hard to learn, and things were about to get much worse before they eventually got better.

George came to the barn. He sounded weary. "Come on you two, time for a walk, I feel like some good fresh air in my lungs, after these last goings on with a certain young pup". I, for one, was glad. I was feeling very frustrated with the behavior of our young rascal.

I knew both my offspring were still in the big barn. Nellie was worried but I tried to tell her that it would do the pair good to learn a bit of discipline. "It will cool them down a bit love, try not to worry."

As we left our barn Harry Potts came round the corner. He shouted loudly "Got your message from the missus George, how can I help?"

I looked at Nellie. What message would that be? Were George and Gertrude
about to give my pups away? Once again that sick feeling returned to my tummy. I tried not to give any indication of my fears to Nellie, but judging by her face, she was thinking along the same lines.

As we left, Harry arrived at George's side. "You say one of your old sheep gave birth to two lambs a couple of weeks ago George?" The old man nodded in response to his friend.

George carried on speaking to Harry. "Come on up the top field and tell me what you think of 'em"

We set off. George had known all along that I was no good with the sheep but, as I said earlier, Gertrude had me because she loves me, despite my bad leg! Anyway, I didn't really like the sheep, I never had.   To me they are just silly big lumps of fluff.

We set off towards the top field. From out of the corner of my eye, I saw Gertrude going towards the big barn that was housing our naughty pups. As she opened the door and without warning Zebedy came flying out. He loved Harry Potts! He had heard the farmer's voice. By now George and Harry were walking by the side of the paddock which was home to Dunk the Donkey, and Lavender the goat.

George often used the enclosure as a short cut to the top field. Well what happened next would go down as the worst thing Zebedy had ever done in his young life so far.

As George lifted the bar on the gate that secured the paddock, young Zeb tongue hanging out, thundered past everyone. He was in his element. With excited barking, common sense out of the window, Zebedy charged at Dunk. He didn't care for this donkey, His constant HE-HAW Really got on the pup's nerves. He would teach Dunk a lesson he wouldn't ever forget.

By now everything was in uproar. George and Gertrude were running round like scalded cats! Nellie was crying, I was barking at my boy. It was mayhem. The next thing to happen gave the young pup the fright of his life. As he went to charge the angry donkey, so Lavender, took the opportunity to teach the young dog a lesson HE wouldn't forget either!. Head down, she charged full pelt at Zebedy.

My parental instinct to the fore, I tried to step in and prevent my son being butted by the now very angry donkey. Unfortunately, I got in the way of the goat's horns. She had entered into the melee, eager to give Zeb a lesson he wouldn't forget in a hurry. I felt the full force of the butt that had been intended for Zeb, right in my bum!

Dunk was He-hawing like crazy. George was shouting, Gertrude was trying to tether the goat. Nellie was crying. Harry Potts took hold of Zebedy. He held him by the scruff of his neck. "Come here you young devil, just look what you've done to Ben."

I had been hurt and it was all the fault of our son! George was examining me. He looked at my rear end, which was hurting rather a lot. After a few gentle prods, George spoke to Gertrude. "I think he will be ok love, a bit sore for a few days around the rump but nothing broken or bleeding."

Well I can tell you I was relieved. That sure was a well aimed butt!   Lavender had paid me back for my tormenting when I was a young un. I was still angry with Zebedy, but how could I be cross with him for long? He was a young dog with cart loads of energy to burn.

Eventually things calmed down. We left the paddock and set off for the top field.
We could see the sheep right at the far end, huddled together, the baby lambs close by.
As George and Harry were talking, Nellie and I walked on ahead. Zebedy, who had been trotting along beside George, tail between his legs, on a short lead suddenly took off, slipping the lead as he did so.

Harry, in hot pursuit, shouted to George, "Don't worry, I'll get the young so and so."

I was really worried now. This was probably the last straw, as far as Zeb was concerned! The young dog seemed absolutely focused on the sheep, and despite the yelling by George, and Harry to "get back here you blasted dog" Zebedy, just kept going.

What happened next, had to be seen to be believed. The young dog without fear, got down on his belly and crawled towards the sheep. They in turn began to run further in the other direction, bleating like crazy.

Zebedy, quick as a flash engineered himself behind them and with expert handling directed the small flock towards us. In no time at all most of the small flock with the two lambs were standing just a few steps away from George with Zeb then bringing up the remaining stubborn old sheep.

George didn't say a word at first, I think he was as shocked as the rest of us, at what we had just witnessed. Harry Potts, after getting his breath back, was the first to speak. "By gum George! The dog is a natural. If I hadn't seen it with my own eyes, I wouldn't have believed it. That's what the young monkey wants, something to run off all that energy. Pity we hadn't realized earlier, it would have saved a lot of hassle with the young devil. How about letting me 'av 'im for a couple of weeks, see if I can train him for ya?"

George by now had just found his voice. "By gum Harry I think you're right lad. I wouldn't have believed that if I hadn't seen it with my own eyes, you had better do that, if you don't mind, after all, if you can't mould him to be the best, then nobody can." To say the men were shocked, by the young pup's performance must be the under-statement of all time.

Gertrude was in tears, Nellie was in tears, and to tell the truth, I could have cried with pride myself. My youngster had done something that I had never been able to accomplish. He had mastered a flock of daft sheep. Little did we know it at the time, but our Zebedy was heading for greatness.

Well things certainly began to take on a different angle. Zebedy went with Harry Potts for a while, to be trained. We missed him, young Evie missed her brother especially, but he wouldn't be away for very long.

Eventually peace returned to Ryder's Ground. Lavender and Dunk had had their day. Hector the goose and Claud the cockerel calmed down now that Zebedy was off their case. My sore rump soon got better. Nellie and I were able to breathe a little easier now that we only had gentle Evie to worry about, well for a short time anyway, and she was no trouble at all.

Mind you Nellie cried a few tears for her son and to be honest I missed the young rascal as well. Unfortunately we were going to miss Zebedy for quite a long time unbeknown to us. For little did anyone know at the time just what was in store for our boy.

CHAPTER TEN

ZEBEDY GOES TO SCHOOL

Nell was very quiet these days. Something seemed to have gone out of her since Zeb had been taken to train as a sheep dog with Harry Potts. Oh, she wasn't worried about Zeb! Not really, we all liked Harry. It was just the missing of the young scallywag that was all. Zeb was such a live wire, always up to some sort of mischief. It was rather quiet nowadays. Even Dunk and Lavender seemed laid back. Evie was missing her brother, probably more than anybody. She was always the one to cover up for him. She would try to protect the young pup when he found some more mischief to get into.

George and Gertrude tried their best to keep things ticking over but I knew they were missing Zeb as well. He was my son, and although he had been a handful right from the time he could walk, I felt the loss very keenly but it was important that I held up for Nellie's sake. After all I was supposed to be the strong one! When my Nellie found it hard to bear, I tried to keep her chin up with words of comfort. "This will be the making of our boy Nell, you will see." What I didn't know at the time was that this was only the start of a much bigger picture.

A few long weeks went by, then we heard some news that was going to change our lives forever.

We had just come back from our evening walk with George, when there was such a commotion. Harry had just brought Zebedy back from his place. On seeing us. the young pup was all over his mother and Evie, jumping and whining with happiness. Nellie was licking her son, like she hadn't seen him in years.

However there was something different about him. Zebedy seemed to have grown up. He pulled himself away from his mum and walked over to where I was. He stood in front of me. Looking confident and self-assured, and in a voice I didn't recognize he said "Hello Dad." Here he was, my boy. I swallowed hard. "Hello my son, you're home then, how was it?"

Zebedy pulled himself up to his full height. "I have a different view of those not so daft sheep now Dad, they are not so much stupid as crafty". Zeb looked me full in the eye. "However they know me, and I know them. Don't give 'em an inch Dad, that's the thing to do."

In the space of a few weeks my son had grown up. I could tell by his mother's attitude towards him that Nellie was taken aback by this change in her boy. I don't think either of us could take in this well-behaved young dog, and as for Evie, she was in absolute awe of her brother.

It seemed that Zebedy had proved his worth, not only for Harry Potts, but so good was he at controlling our neighbours' sheep, he had been brought to the attention of sheep farmers as far away as Lincolnshire and North Wales. There was even a mention of his prowess in the Farmers' Times, it seemed that our boy was being talked about and read about far and wide.

Meanwhile Harry Potts was filling George and Gertrude in with all the news concerning my boy. "He's a blooming natural George, I can hardly believe it, I can tell you now lad, that this dog of yours is in for greatness. You mark my words. Rosettes will be coming out of his ears!"

Nellie and I tried to listen to all that was said between the two men but it was difficult to hear it all. It appeared that our Zebedy was becoming quite famous. It seemed that Harry, not quite expecting our lad to do so well, had phoned George in the first couple of weeks, putting him in the picture as to how well the young dog had done in a couple of sheep trials that had been held on the farm next door to his own property.

It appeared that sheep-dog trainers, who had read the reports in the farming papers had come to witness just what this Wonder Sheep dog was capable of. By all accounts they hadn't been disappointed. Well I can tell you, Nellie and I were over the moon with pride. Our little fire-cracker had made good.

Zebedy stayed on at Ryder's Ground for a few weeks, enabling Nellie, Evie and I to spend time with our boy. Gertrude, especially, made a fuss of him so for a little while Zebedy was seen around the Holding. Dunk and Lavender, couldn't take in the change in my pup, and as for Claud, and Hector, well they couldn't seem to come to terms with this much changed dog either. Between you and me I rather think they missed the arguments. I over-heard Lavender one day complaining to Dunk that Zebedy just wasn't fun anymore!. As for Nellie and I, we were so proud of Zeb for what he had achieved so far. The rosettes Zeb had won were already adorning the sitting room of George and Gertrude, but, things were about to change in a big way. Zebedy's skill with the sheep had travelled far and wide so much so that everyone connected with sheep trials, wanted Zebedy to compete.

So began the life changing activity that would eventually bring about great joy and a certain amount of heart-ache.

CHAPTER ELEVEN

WORKING TOWARDS THE GOAL

"I'm going to a place called Cardigan Bay next Mum, somewhere in Wales George has entered me into a really big show, what do you and Dad think of that? It's the furthest I've been so far, seems its one of the biggest sheep trials yet."   Nellie turned to me and smiled, she was so proud of our Zeb. She nuzzled the young dog's neck. "You will be fine Son just fine, do your very best, that's all you can do" Nellie gave a sigh. "Wish we could see you compete Son, Wales aye. Well I never." I had been thinking along these same lines for some time but realized that the chance of George and Harry taking us to a meeting was out of the question. I nuzzled Nellie, trying to comfort her. "They won't do that love; we would be in the way, besides it's Zebedy' s time now. We must stand back and give him his chance to shine."

Wales! Now that rang a couple of bells and opened up a few memories I would sooner forget. After all a farm in north Wales had been Nellie's and my first home, some memories were ok. Being with Belle and my mum Floss had been wonderful. Hilltop's farm had been my home from my birth.

What hadn't been so good was being sent away to Glenloyd Kennels because Gwyn Thomas, Belle's dad thought me useless because of my bad leg, no good with the sheep you see. He had got rid of my Nellie in the same way just a few weeks before he packed me off to the hell-hole that was Glynloyd Kennels. I had loved Belle so much and I remember with sadness how I felt when ripped away from my home, mum Floss, and Belle. They were memories I didn't like to think about. I sometimes wonder, in my quiet moments, when I'm cleaning my paws or going for a walk with Nellie the pups and George, just how Belle is fairing these days.

I don't suppose much has changed back at Hilltop's? Belle will still be struggling with her bad arm, and Gwyn will be just as miserable. Little did I know at that time, that circumstances were about to change in a big and exciting way. Soon I was to receive a very pleasant surprise, and it was all down to Zebedy. It would dispel once and for all, and put into place everything that had happened in mine and Nellie's life thus far. I recalled my mum Floss telling me a long time ago, that things happen for a purpose. Life was mapped out for us all. Well I can tell you that certain things were about to happen that would put my head in a spin of great happiness so everything that happened to me, including, my leaving Hilltop's, and my stay in Glynloyd, had all been for a purpose.

The said owner of Glynloyd Kennels a certain Jake Binley had treated me and the other inmates in a very cruel way. The only good thing about that terrible place had been Peggy Owen the kennel maid. Unfortunately for the girl, she wasn't treated any better than us dogs!

I remembered with great relief, the way I felt when Binley had got his comeuppance! I recall sometimes with great satisfaction, our friend, the enormous dog Boris chasing Jake Binley and giving him a bite on the bum!

All that was behind me now. As far as I knew Peggy Owen was the owner of the new Glynloyd Kennels, I had heard George and Gertrude discussing the good fortune for the girl some time ago. I secretly wished I could meet Peggy again, but I realized with sadness that this wasn't going to happen!

We said goodbye to George and Zebedy. Our boy was going to the important sheep dog trial in Cardigan Bay. Nellie with tears she was unable to hide nuzzled Zeb, "now be careful my son and do your best. Your dad and I are very proud of you." Zeb nodded to his mother and I. He nuzzled his sister. She missed her brother so much. He spoke with absolute assurance. "Don't worry I will be fine". He nuzzled his mum. I choked back a tear. "Good luck Son, do as your mum says, we will be thinking of you," but I was in for a big surprise.

"Come on Zeb, time to go." It was George. He and Harry Potts, were both going to this important Sheep dog trial. They said goodbye to Gertrude and set off in the old car.
Halfway up the drive, the car stopped, "come on Ben, you can come." It seemed that Harry Potts had persuaded George to take me! Well I can tell you. This was a wonderful surprise. I loved Harry Potts and it was pretty obvious that Harry loved me. I was going to Cardigan Bay to watch my son win a few more rosettes so with a pat from Gertrude, and a nuzzle from Nellie and Evie, I was on my way.

Meanwhile, back at Hilltop's Farm Gwyn and Belle Owen were preparing to go to Cardigan Bay. Belle wondered if this sheep dog trial would be the last for Floss. The old girl had been an inspiration over the past few years, winning rosette after rosette. Floss had given hope and challenge where there was very little. She, as much as anyone had mourned the leaving of her son Ben over all those months ago. Floss understood why Ben had had to go, but to be honest she never really got over the loss of her boy. True, he never would have made a sheep dog bad leg and all, but she thought Gwyn Owen wrong for sending him away, especially for how it had hurt Belle. She knew how much the girl had loved Ben, and to her mind Gwyn had been very wrong to send the young pup away. Belle had needed the dog, after losing her mum in the accident, and at the same time losing her arm. Gwyn had been so wrong, and very cruel.

Floss recalled the tears of anguish poured out by the girl, the first few weeks after his departure. Floss remembered how the girl had hugged her neck, soaking her in tears of sorrow. Both missed the young pup. To her mind, Gwyn Thomas had made a bad mistake sending Ben away to an uncertain future. True, for a long time since sending her boy away, the farmer had been like a bear with a sore head.

Floss reckoned it was probably guilt, especially when he had been unable to placate Belle with anything else. The girl had refused to take to any of his suggestions about taking on a gold fish or a hamster to replace her Ben, for as she told her dad, nothing ever could!

Little did Floss know at this time that certain elements were about to come together. Fate had once again taken a hand in the fortunes of these players in this particular game that was life.

Gwyn Thomas had thrown himself into work. Yes, he did feel bad about sending the young Ben away but his mind had been in a bad place, he neither cared about the girl, the dog, or the farm, for a very long time. Miriam his wife and very best pal had been killed in the car crash, his daughter badly injured so why was he bothered about anything? This was Gwyn Thomas's attitude for a long time but with medication to help him through this harrowing time: and as soon as he began to gather himself once more, the farmer started to see things in a different light. He had started to get back to Sheep-dog trialing. This had been a passion when Miriam was alive. They had travelled all over the country, with Floss. She had always shone in the trials winning rosettes by the handful.

Floss had wondered why, just lately Gwyn had been showing renewed interest in taking her out more, round the sheep, running her and timing the results. Well she was about to find out very soon.

CHAPTER TWELVE

BEST IN SHOW

The old car chugged along the road. It was a long way from Ryder's Ground to Cardigan Bay in Wales. George and Harry were quite excited about the sheep dog trials. This was the big one. They both felt sure that Zebedy would prove himself today. The dog's attitude was right. Harry Potts was double sure of that fact. He knew dogs, and Zebedy was made of that rare and special something.

George had given in to Harry's perseverance. Harry Potts had persuaded him to allow Ben to accompany them to Cardigan Bay. To Harry's mind it would be a good idea. True, Ben had never been sheep dog trialing material, but he was a good lad always a loyal and protective dog to George and Gertrude, making up in a way for not being sheep dog material, and he was a wonderful father figure to Evie and Zebedy. He deserved this treat. "The dog will love it George. Let him see his son perform."

Well, it seemed that my owner had been swayed, agreeing with Harry that I deserved this treat so to my joy the deed had been done and I was travelling with my son to the Sheepdog trials in Cardigan Bay. I suppose, if I told the truth, it would have been nice if Nellie and Evie could have come as well, but I mustn't grumble. Besides I can fill them in when I get back to Ryder's Ground.

Zebedy was quiet. I supposed he would be getting straight in his mind, everything he needed to, concerning this biggest of Trials he had taken part in so far. I didn't suppose I could contribute anything constructive, I had never been in a sheep trial so I didn't know how to help.

After what seemed a very long time, we finally arrived at the trial field. Harry opened the back door of the old car. "Come on you two we're here. Have a drink of water." Harry proceeded to pour the cooling liquid into our bowls. I for one was glad to stretch my now very stiff legs. Zeb, on the other hand, jumped out onto the grass shook himself and seemed ready for anything.

We both had a welcome drink of water. As I looked around this large space, I was overawed at its size. From where we were parked, I could see an enormous building, made of something white with windows, door and a wobbly roof. There was an interesting smell coming from inside the round place. It reminded me of some of the food Gertrude cooked for George sometimes, sausages and onions. There were other smells I wasn't so familiar with. There were lots of people milling around the field, all seeming to talk about those daft sheep. I could see lots of people with food wrapped up in a paper cloth coming out of the round white place.

Harry spoke up next. "How about I go to the tent for a bite to eat, for us both? I think we have time before the first trial". Harry disappeared through a hole in the white building that I now knew was called a tent. He came back carrying a large paper bag, full of something that smelled wonderful. He handed something from the bag to George.
"When did you say it was Zebedy' s turn?"

George, sausage roll in his hand, looked up from his program. "He comes third in line after a dog called Gerard of Cork. He sounds like a hard act to follow."

I was savouring the aroma. I would enjoy a bite of something tasty. Perhaps if I gave Harry that drooling look he would give me a morsel. It had worked in the past, with Harry. He often slipped me a bit of something I wasn't supposed to have. Gertrude was a stickler for feeding us dogs a wholesome diet, as she put it, 'didn't want us to get fat' but I was always glad to see my friend Harry. He often carried tit-bits in his pocket for us. A tasty piece of cheese or a biscuit went down a treat.

Harry must have noticed my 'trying to look starved' attitude. It had worked in the past. Harry put his hand into the bag. He pulled out a small piece of something meaty and was about to pass it to me when George gave Harry that look that said 'no you don't!' He then looked down at Zebedy and I.
"You two can have something to eat when Zebedy has done his trials. No good trying to control a bunch of sheep on a full belly. Why don't you two come and watch the other dogs doing their bit, it will help pass the time until it's Zebedy's turn to do his stuff."

I looked at George, he was quite right of course, but then he usually was. It was important that my boy did his best, for as I understood, from what I had heard Harry and George say, this was the big one.

We both decided to do as George suggested. I for one, just couldn't believe how many people were interested in Sheep dog trials, everywhere I looked there were farmers, shepherds and pens holding bleating sheep.

We then heard an announcement from an important looking man. He was shouting loudly through something in his hand. To me it resembled an empty dog meat tin!!

"LADIES AND GENTLEMEN, he shouted in a very booming voice. "WE NOW HAVE A SPECIAL TREAT FOR ALL YOU TRIALERS. .
AN OLD GIRL, BY THE NAME OF FLOSS, FROM HILLTOP'S FARM, NORTH WALES, WILL BE COMPETING FOR THE LAST TIME...HER OWNER, AND TRAINER BELLE THOMAS, WILL BE GIVING THE COMMANDS.
FLOSS WILL BE SHOWING SOME OF THE YOUNGSTERS, AND UP AND COMING SHEEP DOG TRIALERS, HOW IT SHOULD BE DONE. FLOSS ISN'T COMPETING THIS TIME, IT WILL BE HER LAST PERFORMANCE AS A TRIALER."

There was a thunderous applause. Everyone clapped and cheered. George, who was talking to Harry Potts, looked towards ZEBEDY. "Now watch this boy you are going to see the best." George and Harry had heard all about this special sheep dog but as yet neither had seen her run, well Yorkshire was a long way from North Wales.

As for myself I could hardly believe what I had just heard. Floss's Hilltop's farm, could it really be my Mam? Wasn't I glad that George had let me come to the trials today!   It must have been meant to happen.

From the other side of the field I saw movement. By now everybody had stopped cheering and shouting, the flock of sheep waiting in the pen had become quiet.

Then I saw something that made my tummy turn over. It couldn't be but it was. It was my Mam, and walking onto the field with her was a woman. My heart stopped. Instinct and memory took over.

The lady stopped a few yards away from where we were standing. She motioned to Floss to wait. From the top of the field a man was standing by the sheep pen.
When the woman raised her hand to signal for the sheep to be let out, my mind froze. This lady only had one arm. She was wearing boots, a big coat and a floppy hat, and in her right hand she was holding a whistle, I knew a whistle because George sometimes used one on the daft sheep back home. It was difficult to see her face properly but I was sure it was My Belle!

Belle blew the whistle, and with the command "away Floss" the sheepdog took off.
My legs started to tremble. I wanted to shout out but owing to the importance of the trial I managed to keep quiet. George, with an excited whisper said, "look at her go Harry."

I watched in awe as my mum maneuvered the sheep with skill. When it came to separating the sheep marked with blue ribbon from the others she was absolute magic. She managed to get all the daft sheep into the holding pen, even the one that absolutely refused to do as she was told. I remembered that steely stare! It used to put shivers up me when I was a young pup.

Floss finished with the shedding of the sheep, to a thunderous applause. The old dog had done a wonderful job, a bit slower now but absolutely spot on.

As the shepherdess and dog went to leave the field, they once more passed George, Harry and the two dogs. They were within six yards. Ben with no further ado began to walk towards Floss and Belle.

George, in a loud voice shouted. "Come back here Ben what are you doing?"

Ben just kept on going. He was within a few feet of his mother, and Belle. Tears were beginning to well up in his eyes. Just then. Belle who was in front of Floss, stopped quite still. In a quiet voice she said, "Ben! Is that you boy, is it really you?".

I was looking into the gentle eyes of Belle Thomas. I stood for a split second. Never in a million years had I ever thought this would happen. My mum and Belle were right here where Zebedy was about to perform.

George came up behind me, and grabbed me by the scruff of the neck. In an angry voice, quite out of character he said: "what on earth has got into you lad, have you gone mad, it's almost time for Zebedy to do his stuff, it's his turn next."

For a moment it was as though the earth stood still, I couldn't believe this was happening, but it was. As if this was part of a dream. My Belle came towards me. As she bent down, Belle put her arm around my neck.
  "Ben! My Ben, what are you doing here?"

Well I can tell you, this was something I had never imagined would happen. Belle looked wonderful, she smelled wonderful, sort of homey and familiar, and as for me seeing my mum after all this time?   Well I can tell you, it was unbelievable. To feel the much missed nuzzle of her soft nose in my neck was almost too much to take in. I responded to the much-needed closeness of my mum and Belle.   I thought my tail would wag off. The tears of joy were overwhelming.

I had so much to tell them. How I had missed them both, missed Hilltop's farm, being in the sweet hay with my mum, and how I had been badly treated by Jake Binley. I wanted to tell them about my Nellie, and my lovely life at Ryder's Ground with George and Gertrude and my two pups Evie and Zebedy.

Eventually Belle stood up and wiping her eyes walked towards an astounded George, and Harry while my mum and I, tried to catch up with each other. Belle addressed an irate George. She held out her good hand.
"Hello I am Belle Thomas, from Hilltop's Farm; it was my dad who first had Ben, and through no fault of his own at that moment in time had to send him away". Then she proceeded to put George in the picture. Dad is doing some business at the moment; but he will be here shortly". Looking towards me, she said:
"I am sure you are the one he will be most glad to set eyes on Ben for he is completely recovered from the depression that assailed him for so long." Then with a sad sigh...she said. . "Dad so regrets his treatment of you Ben, I am sure he will be overjoyed to see you again."

Well I can tell you, George's attitude changed in a flash. He along with Harry Potts listened intently to the story, occasionally uttering an expletive swear word or a "well I never." Harry was taking onboard all he had been told. To his and Harry Potts' way of thinking, this sure was some story. The men felt for the girl, she must have suffered a great deal. Losing her mother was bad enough, but to be crippled as well must have taken some swallowing! However, probably, and judging by Belle's tale, the worst loss by far to the girl, was having Ben taken away from her for by everything she told us, her heart had been well and truly broken.

To be honest, the story brought a tear to the eyes of both men. How could the girl's father have been so callous but George and Harry both knew that it takes all sorts to make a world, and after listening to the girl actually defending her father, they surmised that everything is done for a purpose. Besides, by what the girl had told them, the man had been very ill mentally and they knew you didn't get over an illness like that in a short space of time.

As George pointed out to the lass, "if your dad hadn't sent Ben away, we wouldn't be meeting like this today." George liked everything put into its rightful place. To his mind there was a reason for everything, good or bad.

From the corner of the field there came an announcement from the man with the loud haler. We all listened intently to what he had to say.

"Will the owner of Number 3 Zebedy from Ryder's Ground come to the starting point."
The commentator proceeded to give out all Zebedy's achievements thus far.

George excused himself and set off for the starting gate, Zebedy close by his side. All was quiet, then. The crowd seemed to explode. There were cheers, loud clapping, and whistles. This was what the people had come to see, spectators of this wonderful dog's skill, all feeling the need to cheer him on, after that perfect round.

My mum, who by now had gained her composure gave me another nuzzle in my neck.
She asked me, "do you know this dog Ben, I've seen him before at other meetings, he's very good, in a way he reminds me very much of you Son?"

George signaled to the man at the top of the field to open the gate that was holding the sheep.

Zebedy set off with all the skill and dexterity he possessed. George shouted instructions, "come by boy come by". Next, "lie down boy, steady boy steady."

As Zebedy completed each task and instruction from George, you could have heard a pin drop. The last instruction was at the shedding pen.

In the enclosure were five, not so daft sheep, one of them had a blue ribbon around his neck. The task was to separate him from the other four. On the command "open" the gate to the pen was opened, and the sheep were let out.

This task was deemed one of the most difficult to complete in the time allotted.
On command from George, Zebedy set off. The field in question was large, and on a steep slope making the job just that bit harder. All five sheep ran together to the opposite side of the field and out of sight of the many spectators.

A few moments went by, then over the hill came all the sheep, closely followed by Zebedy. What happened next was spectacular. All the sheep stood quite still in a tight bunch. Zebedy was down on his hunkers. He wriggled slowly towards them, concentrating his gaze on the one wearing the ribbon. So great was his authority over them that not one sheep moved, then with the dexterity of a dog that knows just what he's doing, Zebedy got to his feet, and walked slowly towards the flock of sheep. Keeping his eyes trained on the one with the ribbon, he calmly and with confidence got behind her and walked her away from the others and into the pen. Zebedy had completed the Singles course the Driving round and the timed Cross and Pen.

Zebedy had completed his task, and the crowd, who up to now had kept quiet, exploded with gusto.

George and Zebedy walked off the field to thunderous applause. The sheep dog had completed all three Country Shows, England, Ireland and Wales. Now it all depended on the rest of the contestants as to how he had done in this final one for this season. Zebedy and George joined Harry, Ben and the others.

It went without saying that George and Harry were over the moon. Zebedy was the champion in their eyes, no matter what the result. He had competed with the finest sheep dogs in many an event and he may just have won the big one!

Zebedy, puffing and panting, joined the group. He stood in front of his dad. Ben was so full of pride he could hardly speak. He turned slowly towards his mum, and in a voice charged with emotion remarked: "Mum, this is my Son, and your Grandson, Zebedy". Looking towards his boy Ben said, "meet your Grandmother, Floss".

Both dogs stared at each other, and I knew in that instance that something lovely, and beautiful had just taken place. My mum, tears in her eyes, without a bit of shyness, went towards her Grandson, and just said, "I knew it boy I just knew it. You had to be Ben's Son. I felt it deep within me. You so bear his very essence".

George unable to know what was going on, but realizing that something pretty wonderful was taking place, took a good look at Floss. He gave his nose a good blow, and wiped tears from his eyes. He pondered. Could it be, it must be?

Belle, who had taken on board everything that was happening, came to the same conclusion as George Marshall. Zebedy must be Ben's son! , He had to be. The girl called Ben to her side once more. She stroked his curly coat. "Is that what you are trying to tell us lad, that Zebedy is your pup?" Once again she gave me a lovely pat and a cuddle. "You clever boy Ben, well done lad."

I just looked at Belle. I sure was enjoying this turn of events. I didn't blink I just looked into her lovely eyes. They do say that the eyes can speak volumes. People tell me I have lovely eyes very expressive. Well that is very nice to know. I am able to use them sometimes to my advantage! A certain look gets me a treat on occasion. A bit naughty I know but after all I am a dog, and dogs can be very crafty!

Zebedy came and sat down at my side. He had had a surprise as well. Fortunately George was able to put into words to Belle, that which I was unable to do. That yes, Zebedy was indeed Nellie's and my Son! He told the girl all about his sister Evie as well, waiting back home at Ryder's Ground with Gertrude.

I was in for another surprise. How many more could I take?" A voice I never thought to hear again, spoke to me in a tone I wasn't expecting.

"Hello Ben Boy. My; you look fit and well. Real grown up an' all." Then shaking his head as if in disbelief. Gwyn Thomas smiled. "Well I never expected this day to arrive, never in a week of Sundays."

I was looking into the face of the man who all those months ago had sent me off to a very uncertain future. How did I feel? I didn't know at this moment. His face looked kinder, softer, and he sounded different but to be honest, my tummy began to feel unsettled. My last memory of Gwyn Thomas was a rough hand round my neck and a harsh word of dismissal, as I was thrown into the back of a van and driven away from everything and everyone I had known and loved. I wasn't about to forget that experience in a hurry!

I looked up at him. The man looked down at me. Just then, Belle joined her dad.
"Look Dad, it's Ben! Would you ever believe it, doesn't he look so well and have you seen his Son Zebedy. Isn't he a clever dog?"

Gwyn answered his over excited daughter. "Steady on girl! Don't get so carried away, you'll explode in a minute." Gwyn Thomas smiled at me. "Yes I agree Belle, it sure is a surprise. Ben looks absolutely wonderful and to know that the champion sheep dog Zebedy belongs to him is nothing less than fabulous."

Then something happened that I never would have thought could take place in a million years. Gwyn Thomas got down on his knees. He looked into my eyes and with tears welling up, he put his hand out to me, and gently stroked my neck. "Sorry Ben boy. I was in a bad place for a long time, never meant to hurt you lad."

Well. I didn't really understand all the words the man was speaking but I did grasp the sentiment. Dogs do forgive a hurt being done towards them. Dogs are like that you know. I don't like to bear a grudge, it never does to carry on a bad feeling.

I bent my head towards my one time enemy and shuffled close, allowing him to know that all was well with me. Just for a few moments, hurts that had cut so deep, were salved at last. They sort of melted away with the caresses. Man and dog were in perfect harmony once more.

Mind you, it will probably take me a long time to forgive Jake Binley. He did a lot of bad things, not only to me, but other dogs in his care. It will be hard to come to terms with the cruel treatment he doled out to poor Peggy Owen. However, I suppose I had better work towards thinking better thoughts of that particular fellow. After all he did get a certain comeuppance with that bite on his bum from Boris! My goodness, I think I heard those screams uttered from his mouth for a long time, it really served the bully right. I was never going to forget that, never. It certainly had been payback time for him.

Besides. perhaps we have to go down certain paths in order to reach our happy home. Good and bad, life's experiences make us what we are. I remember Mum telling me that fact, when I had an argument with Dunk the Donkey and Lavender the Goat when I was a naughty young pup. I remember I used to like to torment the dopey things! When I got a hard butt in my backside, it served me right. I learned my lesson, the hard and very painful way!

Eventually the sheep dog trials came to an end. It had been a wonderful day. Friendships had been rekindled. I had met my mum and Belle, and made my peace with Gwyn Thomas. George Harry, Belle and Gwyn, made arrangements to keep in touch in the future.

George and Harry were preparing to go back to Ryder's Ground, I felt rather sad in a way. The sheep dog trial had meant me finding my mum and Belle. It was wonderful to be in touch again after almost two years, and as for making my peace with Gwyn, it was lovely but I knew that returning home would mean me missing my mum and Belle all over again. That was going to be hard but I was in for another pleasant surprise.

George was talking to Gwyn. The two men were deep in conversation. They pointed first to Floss, then towards the car. I had been put into the back seat along with Zebedy. I wasn't looking forward to leaving my mum and Belle. We seemed to wait for ages. Then, came a surprise. George opened the car door. He had put my mum's collar and lead into the car beside me. What was going on? All of a sudden Belle called to Zebedy who by now was curled up beside me on the back seat of George's car.

Zebedy looked up at me. "What do you suppose Belle wants me for Dad?" We were soon to find out. All of a sudden, my mum jumped in beside me, then Belle called again. "Zebedy come on boy, you're coming to Hilltop's for a while." I looked at my mum for the answer.

She tried to placate me by telling me not to worry but this was strange. Then Belle came to the car. "It's alright Ben. Dad and George decided to try something. Floss is going to stay with you at your small-holding in Yorkshire and Zebedy is coming home to Hilltop's with us for a while. We will meet up again soon. Don't fret yourself boy, your pup will be just fine."

I settled myself. If Belle said it was alright, then it must be. Goodbyes were said, and we were off. It was lovely to snuggle up to my mum again, but I sure was going to miss Zebedy and Belle, and what about Nellie and Evie. How would they react to Zeb being taken so far away? I suppose I should be used to changes, for that is the way of it when you're a dog but all the same, I don't have to like it!

We arrived back at Ryder's Ground. Gertrude greeted us at the door. I think she was very surprised to see my mum instead of Zebedy. George settled Mum and I into the barn. Then he went into the house to explain to Gertrude just what had happened.

Mum and I had mixed feelings. It was lovely to be together, but Mum had to get used to a different set of rules, and I had to feel the loss of my boy. As for Evie and Nellie, the missing of Zebedy was hard to take but very soon, my mum was in her element. She was able to give her new-found granddaughter Evie her loving attention. To my Nellie, she gave the benefit of her wisdom. Mum was good at that.

Mum remembered Nellie being sent away from Hilltop's farm a few months before me, when she was a little pup. It soon became obvious that Mum liked my Nellie. I was glad about that.

We all settled down, to the new way of things. It was two weeks since the change, Zebedy being sent to Hilltop's, and my mum coming to stay with us. Gertrude became very fond of her, I heard her telling George she liked Floss, she said she was a good old girl.

I introduced Mum to the other residents of Ryder's Ground, and strangely enough Lavender, and Dunk liked her. These two tolerated me these days. As for Claud and Hector, well this pair of birds gave her a wide berth! Perhaps Mum had given them one of her, 'don't you dare' stares! I remembered those from my own puppy days. They were enough to turn milk sour. I thought on them with trepidation.

To tell the truth I loved Mum being here at Ryder's Ground, she seemed to have settled down well to the quieter life. She told me the other day that it had started to be too much for her on her own at Hilltop's farm. "My old legs aren't as good as they used to be Son, I'm past it now. Perhaps it is time for young Zebedy to show Gwyn Thomas just what he's made of."

Oh, I still miss Zebedy, and I know his mother misses him. I still hear my Nellie shedding a tear when she thinks I'm out of earshot but it seems our boy is doing well at Hilltop's Farm. From what Nellie, Mum and I can work out, Zeb is doing such a good job with the sheep, that Gwyn Thomas finds him invaluable.

I overheard George on the telephone the other day. He was talking to Gwyn Thomas about Zebedy.
"You say he is the best dog you've ever seen Gwyn, since Floss was a young dog, and you'd like to buy him, hang on a moment, while I go and have a word with my wife."

Then there was a long pause. After a while, the old man was in deep conversation with Gertrude. She replied in a worried voice. "Don't know George, Zebedy belongs to us, how do we know he likes it in Wales, Don't you think he will miss his life at Ryder's Ground with us?"

George answered his wife, "well according to what Gwyn Thomas tells me, the young dog loves it, miles and miles of open fields, and sheep to take care of. The farmer says our Zebedy is in his element love. The thing is, can we stand in his way Gert, it may be the young dog's destiny. You've heard all the talk Lass, we have counted the rosettes he's won, can we really stand in his way because we can't bear the thought of him not being with us anymore?"

George knew what was really on Gertrude's mind. She was finding it hard to let go. Zebedy had been a live wire when a pup but he had wrapped himself well and truly around the old lady's heart. Partings were hard to bear, but sometimes they need to be borne. It would be in the interest of Zebedy to give him his wings, so to speak, allowing him the destiny he deserved.

Well it seemed, that after a good talk with George, and a personal telephone call to Gwyn Thomas, reminding the farmer to take proper care of our Zebedy and that no payment was required, Gertrude had accepted the inevitable, that staying on the large sheep farm in Wales would be the best thing for Zebedy.

Eventually, life at Ryder's Ground settled down to something resembling normality.
Oh we all missed young Zeb, but we had to accept the inevitable. Mum was put in charge of the few sheep in the top field, George said he thought it was better for her to keep her hand in. "Not too stressful for the old girl." Well that's what I heard him telling Harry Potts. Mum took to the small job very well. Evie and I like to go with her. Evie loves her Gran, as much as I do so life is quite sweet at the moment. My Nellie talks a lot to my mum, they talk about female dog things that I know nothing about.

Things had moved on a pace. By now it was early summer, the sky was blue, things at Ryder's Ground were running very smoothly. George all excited told us that Zebedy had won a best in show award once again. He had read a report in the Farmers' Times newspaper. I didn't understand much of what he was saying but I got the enthusiasm in his voice when he spoke of my boy.

Nellie was very proud of her son also. She still missed him, as we all did, but sometimes you just have to get on with it. Even us dogs know that! Besides, since my mum came to live with us, it was as if Nellie had someone who really understood her feelings, probably girls together stuff!

Gertrude came to our Pen in the barn, we had just finished our morning work. The sheep had been brought down to the bottom field.

"How about a day in Whitby, we haven't been for a long time, I'm sure Floss will like it there, do you remember Ben when we took you and Nellie some time ago?"
Well I can tell you. I froze, I remembered alright! That was the place where the sky came down to the biggest duck pond I had seen in my entire life, and my Nellie had been made very tired, fat and grumpy! Did I want to go again?

Well it seemed I was to be outnumbered. My mum said she would like to go to THE SEASIDE whatever that was! Gertrude was ready with her bucket and spade. Evie caught up in the enthusiasm said she would like to go so that was that.

The next morning, after George had handed over the reins of Ryder's Ground to Harry Potts for the day, we were off to Whitby.

Well even I had to admit, that it was quite nice. We had been before so I knew what to expect. The journey was interesting with lots of fields to see on the way. There were sheep and cows watching us as we passed. There were no cows at Rider's Ground but I had seen them on Harry Potts' Farm. He had a few of the big lumpy, noisy things.

These cows didn't like me much, and I didn't like them. The one called Daisy always eyes me up and down whenever Harry takes me onto his farm. I stay well clear of her. She has horns similar to Lavender's, even bigger than the goat's and I know to my cost how a butt from them gave me a bruised bum when I was a pup! Dogs don't forget in a hurry.

We arrived at the seaside. George drove the car onto the soft stuff. I wondered what my mum and Evie would make of the powdery sinky floor.

Gertrude was first out of the car. She opened our door. "Come on you dogs, we've arrived.

Floss looked beyond Gertrude at the scene before her, and then at me. "What is it Ben, you were right about the big duck pond, I've never seen a bigger one." We all got out of the car. Nellie and I were used to the feeling of the soft stuff but Evie and my mum just stood and stared. Mum spoke, "you were right Son. The duck pond does go as far as the bottom of the sky."

I set off. I was going to show Mum that it was nothing to be scared of. Nellie followed close behind me. The soft stuff was nice and warm. George and Gertrude were taking their shoes and socks off. Evie yelled out, "look! Gertrude's feet have been swallowed by the soft stuff, she's sinking." The old lady began to laugh. "Oh Evie, it won't hurt me or you, come on with me."

Floss, who by now was getting used to the feeling began to walk towards the 'duck pond.' "Look" she cried. "My paws have gone as well." As she got closer to the water, the soft stuff seemed to change texture. She called out to the rest of them. "Come on, it's fine for walking down here now. I'm going for a drink."

Before George or Gertrude could stop her, Floss had reached the shoreline and was taking a big drink. Well, I thought my mum was going to choke! She spluttered, and coughed. "This doesn't taste like our duck pond water at home, it tastes horrible, no wonder there aren't any ducks swimming on it"!

Gertrude yelled from the car. "I brought you a bowl and bottle of water from home, that is salt water, it's the North Sea you're drinking, you silly dog."

My mum still spluttering and coughing went towards Gertrude. I bet she felt a bit silly. After a little while we all calmed down. Gertrude put us all some biscuits in our bowls, she gave George some bread and cheese, and we all tucked in.

After a few runs on the soft stuff with a big ball, we all went for a paddle. My mum wasn't all that keen, I think the thought of drinking that horrible water had put her off having anything else to do with the horrible tasting muck!

As we played, Evie let out a yell, "Look! The horrible water is chasing us, quick Dad run! I'm going back to Gertrude." George who was really getting into the ball game let out a raucous laugh.

"It's only the tide coming in you silly dog, it won't hurt you but Evie kept on running until she reached the safety of Gertrude's cuddle. Well we all laughed, but to be honest, I didn't like this duck pond very much, it was far too big and it made funny noises, it smelled funny, and I saw some funny creatures moving about in it!

We stayed at the seaside until George said it was time to go home. Well I wasn't sorry. Running about had made my bad leg ache. I didn't want to make a fuss, dogs don't you know. We just get on with it. I remember George telling Gertrude once when I was limping rather badly. "Well he's still like a baby love, likes the attention." I remember Gertrude's answer: "just like all men" but I don't believe for one minute she was being unkind, 'cause she smiled when she said it.

We had been back from the seaside for about five weeks, when I noticed Nellie was getting very grumpy again she was also getting fat. She seemed to be spending a lot of time with my mum. They were talking about private things that I didn't understand. So I spent as much time as I could with Evie, she had noticed the change in Nellie. "What's the matter with Mum, she doesn't seem to want me around at the moment." George took us up to the top field with him and Harry Potts. They knew what was going on, George just said in a very knowing way: "best to keep out of the way dogs, it's women's work again".

I stopped in my tracks. Women's work! I had heard that remark before, and it was after we had been to the seaside before. It had happened again. The seaside had made my Nellie fat and bad tempered last time we went. It was happening again! We were never going there again ever!

The next thing to happen put Nellie's changing attitude into the back of my mind. There was great excitement at Ryder's Ground. George had received a phone call from Gwyn Thomas. It seemed, from what I could gather, that Zebedy, Belle and Gwyn were coming to visit in a week or two.

Well I can tell you that everybody was excited. We hadn't seen our boy for a few months. He had been busy travelling around to different sheep-dog shows. He had apparently been as far as somewhere called Scotland. He had finished the trials and was coming to visit us.

It would be nice to see Belle again. I loved her. It was a comfort to me that my boy was experiencing the same sort of care that I had always received from this wonderful girl.

Nellie showed some interest in her son coming home but by now she was as fat as pudding and feeling rather fed up with herself. She seemed to be sleeping a lot of the time, and fidgeting about the rest of the time.

Gertrude was busying herself with getting everything ready for the arrival of her guests. The pen next to Nellie's, Evie's and mine was made ready. Fresh hay and a warm blanket were put in readiness for the important occupant. I could hardly wait for our visitors to arrive.

About mid-morning after we had been to the top field, a big van arrived in the yard. Gwyn Thomas was the first to jump out, followed by Belle. She came over to me while Gwyn opened the back door of the vehicle. Well I can tell you everything went mad. I was barking, and almost wagging my tail off, Zebedy was doing the same. Little Evie was trying her best to get to her brother. Belle was hugging and kissing me. Gertrude was wiping her eyes with her duster. George and Gwyn shook hands. Everyone was talking and barking all at once.

I thought I would burst with pride. My son walked towards me. "How are you Dad, where's Mum?" Evie piped up. "Mum's all fat and tired, she's resting as usual."

Zebedy looked concerned. "What do you mean Evie, is Mum alright? I must go and see her." Just then from across the yard, Gertrude called out. "George go and get Mr. Price, I think it's Nellie's time." I held my breath and looked at Zebedy, Mr. Price was the vet. I remembered he only came to Ryder's Ground if one of us animals was ill, or needed our injections which I hate! The needle under the skin isn't supposed to hurt, but it sometimes does, I usually disappear when worming time comes round. Those tablets are too big to swallow. Gertrude usually finds me though!

George rushed towards the house. In no time at all he was explaining to the vet, all about my Nellie, and what he thought was wrong. I overheard him say the word pregnant. I held my breath again. I was recalling that word! The same thing had happened last time we went to the seaside.

That was it! I was never going to that place again. I couldn't let Nellie go through all this fat grumpy tiredness again.

Zebedy was by now very anxious to see his mother so we all trooped towards the Barn. When we arrived I was taken back to the last time this had happened. The same smell, the same squeaking squealing snuffles. Noises that meant only one thing! Zebedy was the first to get to the pen, closely followed by me. Gertrude, and George were on the floor, kneeling over Nell, so was the vet. "Good girl Nellie, just one more push." What did Mr. Price mean "Just one more push?" Who was pushing who?"

Zebedy, stepped forward, and getting down on his belly he crawled towards his mother. At that very moment Nellie gave a huge gasp. "Zebedy, is that really you my son?" Zebedy nuzzled his mother's neck, "Yes it's me Mum I've come home for a while." At that precise time, and with a last groan from Nellie, came the familiar sound of new life.

Nellie had given birth to two pups. "There's a good girl Nellie, a pigeon pair. One of each." George was over the moon. Gertrude as usual, when anything momentous happened, was crying into her pinny.

Mr. Price was talking to George and Gertrude. "I think they had better be the last litter for the old girl, she's a bit past it now. Would you like me to make sure?" George nodded his head to Mr. Price. The vet replied. "Bring her to my surgery when she's recovered, and I will attend to the little job." George nodded once more with a "will do Vet."

We sometimes went to see Mr. Price, he pressed our tummies and put something tickly in our ears. Glad he didn't want to see me this time!

Yes, if I could speak I would tell George that on no account would we want to go to the seaside again. In fact it was never suggested. I would bark my head off in defiance, and refuse to go. Nellie had had enough of these squirming pups eating her tummy! The thought of another episode like this was beyond thinking about. SEASIDE meant more pups. My Nellie had had enough I was putting my paw down.

Zebedy, Belle and Gwyn stayed for a few more days, promising a return visit in the near future. It was lovely to spend time with Belle and Zebedy especially.

Nellie was as usual a wonderful mother to her latest pups young Peg and Billy. Peg is the image of her mother, and Billy is just like me. Well that's what George and Gertrude think. I must say I agree with them. For at about three months old my Nellie's youngest pups are very handsome.

Billy is a live wire, into everything. He reminds me of Zebedy when he was a young un! Gertrude gave Peg her name, just because she liked it. I was glad of this.

Her namesake Peggy Owen this down trodden girl was a wonderful friend to me when I first arrived at Glynloyd Kennels. She tried to make up with kindness, what horrible Jake Binley did with cruelty to us dogs in his care so the name Peg was to hold a warm remembrance in my heart of a true friend.

But that chapter in my life was over long ago. I tell myself that everything in life happens for a purpose. I remember my mum telling me those words a long time ago.

CHAPTER THIRTEEN

COMING FULL CIRCLE

As time marched on, Belle Gwyn and Zebedy came to visit us on a regular basis, Zebedy taking our Billy under his wing so to speak. Zeb was wonderful older brother material for the young 'fire cracker' as George calls him, and who knows perhaps the young Billy will grow up to be a champion Sheepdog like his brother Zebedy.

As for Nellie and I, well, we just sit back and thank our lucky stars that fate had truly lead us home. I have travelled many miles these last couple of years. My life has been touched by sorrow and deep joy. I felt sorrow that I had been torn away from everything I loved when I was very young, worried that I would never again see my mum or Belle.
The others, who have crossed my path, during this time of change, who made an impression on my life, for good or bad, show us that all experiences are building blocks and in the end make us what we are. Nellie and I came through so much pain, to bring us to where we are now, a place that has wrapped itself around our hearts, for we all perceive, deep in our being, just what home really means. A place of comfort! A place of peace! A place, where you truly belong!   Along many winding different roads, roads that eventually lead us home.

The end.